STRIKER

THE
EDGE

NICK HALE

EGMONT

Special thanks to Michael Ford
To Sara G, a dynamite Number 9

EGMONT
We bring stories to life

Striker: The Edge first published in Great Britain 2011
by Egmont UK Limited
239 Kensington High Street, London W8 6SA

Text copyright © Working Partners Ltd 2011
Series created by Working Partners Ltd

The moral rights of the author have been asserted

ISBN 978 1 4052 5685 8

3 5 7 9 10 8 6 4 2

A CIP catalogue record for this title is available
from the British Library

Typeset by Avon DataSet Ltd, Bidford on Avon, Warwickshire
Printed and bound in Great Britain by the CPI Group

Mixed Sources
Product group from well-managed
forests and other controlled sources
www.fsc.org Cert no. TT-COC-002332
© 1996 Forest Stewardship Council

FSC

Egmont is passionate about helping to preserve the world's remaining ancient forests.
We only use paper from legal and sustainable forest sources, so we know where every
single tree comes from that goes into every paper that makes up every book.

This book is made from paper certified by the Forestry Stewardship Council (FSC),
an organisation dedicated to promoting responsible management of forest resources.
For more information on the FSC, please visit **www.fsc.org**. To learn more about
Egmont's sustainable paper policy, please visit **www.egmont.co.uk/ethical**.

STRIKER

THE
EDGE

NICK HALE

1

In the intense Florida sunshine and muggy air, Jake felt as if he was slowly suffocating. He checked his watch, the silver Rolex bringing a flashback of a face he'd rather forget. Igor Popov, the billionaire Russian crime lord, had given it to him as a sarcastic 'thank you' for Jake's efforts in bringing down one of Popov's enemies. Jake wore it as a reminder that he had a score to settle.

One day . . .

But not today. Today was not about Russian gangsters or international intrigue. If his dad could take a break from the spy game, then so could Jake. Jake noticed the time and pushed revenge to the back of his mind. If he didn't hurry, he'd be late.

The main stadium, fifteen metres high with tiers of stands on three sides, loomed in front of Jake. Beyond the stadium was the rest of the Olympic Advantage Complex − or the

Ares Sports Olympic Advantage Complex, to use its full name. Nestled between the sprawling Everglades National Park and the town of Redford, the complex covered twenty acres of old swampland.

For the next two weeks, Olympic Advantage would control everything about Jake's life: his schedule, sleep patterns, nutrition. Even with the gruelling schedule and epic rule book, Jake felt like pinching himself. This was a once-in-a-lifetime opportunity.

A couple of athletes sped past Jake, as if he was standing still. He recognised one as Theo, an Italian in his dorm block. Jake had attended a couple of international schools, but the mix was never this diverse. So far at Olympic Advantage he'd met a cyclist from Canada, a Kenyan runner and a gymnast from Russia. Jake shared a room with Tan Wu, a decathlete from China. He hadn't met the rest of the footballers yet, but the brochure said they'd be the best from around the globe.

Excellence was the minimum requirement.

Jake broke into a run past Theo and the other boy, through the tunnel and into the stadium, and couldn't help but gasp. It was pristine: freshly laid turf, bordered by a perfect running track that shimmered in the sun. Workmen were scattered around, putting the finishing touches to the lighting rigs and technical areas, in preparation for the opening ceremony later that day. A couple of suits stood up in the stands, deep in conversation. Jake recognised one as the camp director Bruce Krantz, four-time-Gold Australian rowing champion. Perhaps the other was one of the international investors with big brands on the lookout for future stars. The word in the dorms, probably exaggerated, was that some of the athletes would be leaving with contracts worth hundreds of thousands of dollars.

Jake made for the crowd gathered at the far end of the stadium, taking the running track in long strides. An Olympic Edge banner flew above the cluster of athletes, and they were surrounded by lighting equipment and huge stationary cameras. He had been selected to star in a commercial for Olympic Edge, a new performance-aiding sports drink manufactured by the camp's main sponsor: LGE. He didn't even want to be in the stupid commercial. All he wanted to do was play world-class football. He didn't like all the politics and marketing, but he'd learned from his dad that it was all part of the game.

'Hey, you,' said the director, a skinny guy whose accent was pure Brooklyn. 'Thanks for joining us. Stand over there by the blonde, will ya?'

'My name's Veronika,' the girl said to the director, spinning a tennis racket in her hand. 'As I've told you twice before.'

'Whatever, sugar,' he replied.

Jake smiled, taking his position beside the tanned American girl. *He* certainly wouldn't be forgetting Veronika Richardson's name. She'd won last year's junior Wimbledon, and was tipped to be in the top twenty by the end of her first pro season. Up until that moment, he hadn't dared go near her. With her long blonde hair, incredible legs and model looks, she was the definition of unapproachable.

'The guy's an idiot,' he said to her.

Veronika looked him up and down, but said nothing.

'Jake,' he said, holding out his hand.

She left him hanging. 'I have a boyfriend,' she replied, and pointedly turned away.

Jake was about to protest his innocence when the director shouted out, 'Right, I want all of you together in a group. Act like you're having fun, and like you *wouldn't* kill your roommate for a shot at one of those big sponsorship contracts.'

The Olympic Advantage hopefuls came together, as instructed. A team of young women with make-up brushes at the ready descended on the group. Jake tried to protest, but everyone was getting the same make-over treatment. They didn't lay a brush on Veronika.

Jake found himself between two athletes whose differences were almost comical: his roommate Tan Wu, five-seven and not an ounce of fat on him, and Otto Kahn, a mountainous German weightlifter. Jake reckoned the circumference of Otto's biceps was larger than Jake's quads. He'd seen him in the canteen that morning, and counted the seventeen pancakes that he'd put away . . . *after* the three bowls of cereal.

The director finally called 'action' while they all pretended to be enjoying themselves. Otto told a joke in his broken English about his father putting out his back carrying 'baby Otto' to keep them laughing.

After the director yelled, 'Cut!', they were each given a bottle of Olympic Edge, ready for close-ups. Jake held the 'Riptide' flavour, which was sickly blue. Others had red, white, green or yellow drinks. Different flavours, but all with stupid names. Jake saw that the red one Veronika held was called 'Magma'. When the director told them the advertising hook-line, they all groaned in unison.

'Whine all you like, but they're paying a lot of money for you to be here,' the director said. Jake was about to complain to Veronika, thinking it might get a reaction, but Otto was already sidling up.

'That line is so corny, isn't it?' the big German said.

'Like your pick-up lines,' she answered, walking away.

Jake slapped Otto on the shoulder. 'Don't worry, big fella – I got turned down myself.'

Otto's face split into a grin as he watched her speaking with the Pakistani long-jumper, Ree. 'She's very tough,' he said.

'Pretty boy!' The director clicked his fingers at Jake. 'You're up. On cue, take a long swig, kick your ball, then say the line.'

Jake nodded.

'Ready . . . Action.'

Jake took a gulp of Olympic Edge, and immediately spat it out on the grass.

'Cut!' shouted the director. 'What the hell was that?'

'It's disgusting!' Jake said. 'It tastes like petrol mixed with spinach.'

The director clicked his fingers at his sweaty assistant. 'We'll come back to you, and you can try one of the other flavours,' the director said, and then whispered something to his assistant that sent her running.

Otto laughed at Jake and chugged down his bottle of white Olympic Edge, called 'Lightning'. 'I like it,' he told Jake.

Jake passed over his bottle of 'Riptide'. 'It's all yours. But I can't imagine how you can drink that stuff.'

'You learn to like it,' Otto said, suddenly serious. 'Three times a day, for a whole two weeks. The sponsor's rules. You do not want to upset the moneymen.'

'They can't *make* us drink it, can they?' Jake asked.

Otto finished Jake's bottle and aimed for a bin. He missed.

'Basketball not my sport,' he said glumly.

Jake and Otto watched as the other athletes swigged and smiled for the camera. Veronika made it look effortless. She took a sip of 'Magma', then swung her tennis racket in a backhand action, before tossing her hair over her shoulder as she delivered the line. Tan performed his takes while hurling a discus. When Jake's turn came round again, he was told off because his hand obscured the label. He managed to fake the gulping part, taking the tiniest of sips. Then he flicked up the football and volleyed into the goal in one take. He didn't fluff the line. To his frustration, Veronika was looking the other way, miming tennis shots.

'Right,' the director said, snapping his fingers at Otto. 'You're last, Chunky.'

Otto came up, grabbing a new bottle of Olympic Edge – it was yellow and looked like urine. Jake made out the name 'Solar'. On the ground in front of Otto was a fifty-kilogram barbell.

'You know the drill,' the director said.

Otto nodded. At the action call, Otto guzzled down half the bottle, which he then crushed with one hand. He crouched and gripped the bar. In a single squat and thrust he hoisted it over his head.

7

'Olympic Edge gives . . .' His voice gave out and his knees seemed to wobble. Jake knew straight away that something was wrong.

'Cut!' snapped the director. 'Come on, Tubbs, it's a simple line.'

But Otto's arms were trembling too. Jake saw his skin had suddenly drained of colour.

'Help him!' Jake shouted, and tried to push past the onlookers and crew.

Otto staggered to one side. As he went down on a knee, the bar jerked aside. The weights at one end crashed into his shoulder, and Otto's head was pushed hard into the turf.

Ree screamed, and someone shouted for a doctor. Jake rushed to Otto's side. The bar was resting over the boy's neck, compressing it hideously.

'Get it off him!' Jake shouted. 'Help me!'

Tan joined him at one end and a Dutch swimmer called Anders took the other. On a count of three, they heaved and managed to pull the weight clear of Otto's neck. But Jake could see that Otto was dead.

2

D r Chow, the camp's Chinese-American head of research, hurried past one of the cameras.

'Nobody move him,' she ordered.

'Maybe he no warm up right,' Tan whispered, backing away.

Jake disagreed with Tan. Otto had been lifting for years. Surely he would have known his limits.

Dr Chow knelt beside the body and tried to check Otto's pulse in his mangled neck. She obviously couldn't find one, because she went to his wrist next. Jake couldn't take his eyes off Otto. There was a vivid red abrasion where the bar had grazed his skin beneath his jawline, and his neck was twisted like a wrung towel. Jake guessed that his vertebra had been snapped. If so, at least he wouldn't have felt anything.

Dr Chow stood up slowly, and reached for one of the Olympic Advantage flags that was lying around for the commercial shoot. She pulled it over Otto's body.

Bruce Krantz jogged up in his suit. His eyes widened when he saw the body.

'What happened?'

'An accident,' Dr Chow said matter-of-factly. 'Otto Kahn is dead.'

Krantz ran a hand over his shaven head. He pulled his companion – the guy Jake thought might be a sponsor – aside, and together they spoke with Dr Chow.

I was joking with him less than five minutes ago.

A Jamaican sprinter called Dom had his arms round Ree, and she was crying into his chest. At last, Jake heard a distant ambulance siren. *No hurry*, Jake thought grimly. Veronika stood alone to one side, very still. She was the only one not staring at the body.

Krantz broke away from the group, talking on a mobile phone: '. . . We can't go ahead with the ceremony after this. We'll get a statement out within the hour . . .'

Jake realised his arms ached. He must have pulled muscles trying to shift the barbell, the adrenalin of the moment hiding it from him.

'The rest of you, back to your rooms,' Krantz said, shutting off his phone. 'I know it'll be hard to forget . . .' His tone suddenly softened. 'Er . . . I'll post some details in the administration block about grief counselling. I don't want anyone to feel they can't come to me with their problems. But, please, I can't stress this enough, don't talk to *anyone* outside the complex.'

Jake's phone buzzed and he pulled it out of his pocket. His dad's number. He couldn't take it now. Not when all this was happening around him. He put it away, letting the call go to answerphone.

As Jake was walking away with his roommate, Dr Chow called after him.

'Jake, don't forget your physical this afternoon,' she said.

'The show must go on,' Jake muttered so that only Tan heard.

'One death not enough to close the camp,' said Tan, shaking his head.

They joined Ree and Dom and made their way out of the stadium as the ambulance drove straight across the middle of the new pitch. Outside, a tree-lined path led to the dormitory buildings and canteen. Surrounding the stadium were more sports pitches of all descriptions — tennis courts, an Olympic-size swimming pool and a lake for sailing. Beside the football practice pitch were the medical centre and physio rooms, where Jake was due to meet Dr Chow after lunch. The whole complex was surrounded by a wire fence. Apparently the Everglades to the south were infested with alligators.

'Do you think they might send us home?' Dom asked.

Jake shrugged.

'I don't understand,' Ree said. 'He seemed so strong. So *healthy*.'

'Maybe it was drugs,' Dom said. 'A boy shouldn't be so big. Maybe steroids. Or maybe –'

'I think we should not say these things,' Tan interrupted. 'It is too soon to know.'

Jake's phone went again. His dad. He had promised to stay in a hotel in neighbouring Miami. Even a whiff of Bastin Senior at Olympic Advantage and Jake knew any chance he had of making a name for himself, based on his own skill, would be lost. Jake drifted away from the rest of the group. 'Hey, Dad,' he started, but his dad didn't let him finish.

'Thank God, Jake. Are you all right? Why didn't you answer?'

'I'm fine, Dad, but –'

'I was worried sick. I heard a report that a young male athlete had been badly injured at Olympic Advantage.'

'He's dead, Dad,' said Jake. 'It was horrible.' He told his father what had happened, but another part of his mind was wondering how his dad had found out so quickly. They couldn't have despatched a press statement in such a short time. He doubted even Otto's parents had received the awful news yet.

'Are you spying on me?' he asked.

'What? No,' his dad said. 'I just keep my ear to the ground, that's all.'

'And does MI6 keep tabs on Olympic Advantage?' Jake whispered into the phone.

'They keep an eye on any international gathering of this calibre.' His dad paused. 'Yes, all right. I asked them to keep me informed if anything unusual happened. With everything that's gone on in the last few months . . . I'm just worried about you.'

'Well, you don't have to be,' Jake said. 'It was an accident. And I think I've proved I can take care of myself.'

This was no overstatement. In the last few months, Jake had discovered his dad was a spy for MI6, he'd teamed up with him to apprehend a murdering father and son in Russia and stopped a diamond tycoon's killing spree. Death and destruction had seemed to hunt Jake, but he'd dodged them as skilfully as he'd ridden bad challenges on his school football field.

'OK, son,' his dad said. 'You be careful. And enjoy yourself. In that order. Understood?'

'Understood.' Jake spotted Veronika leaning against a wall off to one side of the stadium. The others didn't seem to have noticed her. 'I've got to go.'

He hung up and walked towards her. They might have got

off on the wrong foot, but she must be as traumatised as the rest of them by what had happened.

He was twenty metres away when a black Mercedes 4x4 pulled up beside her. Veronika stood straighter, but didn't move as the doors popped open. Three white guys, all in suits, stepped out. One faced her, the other two flanking.

'Hey, Tan,' Jake called over without taking his eyes off Veronika. 'Come here, would you?'

The lead man tried to take Veronika's hand and kiss it, but she pulled it away. He spread his arms and began speaking, but Jake wasn't close enough to hear. She shook her head, and the man said something to his friend. All three started laughing, and he reached again, this time grabbing the top of her arm and pulling her towards the car. Veronika jerked free.

Tan arrived at Jake's side.

'Veronika's got trouble,' Jake said.

As they watched, Veronika unleashed a vicious slap across the man's face. All three stopped laughing. Jake expected them to retaliate, but nothing happened. The man smiled and spoke again. He pulled open his jacket, which Jake thought was an odd gesture until he caught a glimmer of gun-metal inside.

3

As quickly as he'd flashed the weapon, he covered it again. How had they got past security? Olympic Advantage had armed guards at the gates.

Veronika didn't seem impressed, and cocked her chin.

Jake strode over with Tan in tow. 'Follow my lead,' Jake muttered, then called out: 'Hi, Veronika, you coming to get that pizza?'

Veronika's face creased in confusion. The three men stared at Jake with a complete lack of interest.

'What pizza?' she said. 'We're not allowed *pizza*.'

Jake paused. *Is she naturally difficult, or just dumb?*

'Y'know,' said Jake. 'That high-protein, slow-burn carb one the nutritionist was going on about.' He tapped his watch. 'It's ready, like, *now*.'

'Too good to miss!' Tan added, playing his part to perfection.

Veronika's eyes widened for a fraction of a second. 'Oh,

yes! Right.' She brushed past the man at her side, and he said something in a language Jake didn't recognise.

'Don't count on it,' Veronika replied.

The guys climbed back into the 4x4 and drove away at a crawl.

'Who was that?' Jake asked.

'Mind your own business,' Veronika said, stalking off.

'Hey!' Jake called. 'How about a thanks for the save?'

She spun round, walking backwards and flashing a smile. 'I don't need saving.'

A few hours later, Jake stood in a tiny bathroom cubicle, wondering if humiliation was part of the Olympic Advantage experience. A guy was waiting for him on the other side of the door.

Trouble was, knowing this made it even harder to go.

'You all right in there?' said the guy, his accent American. 'There's a line, y'know.'

'All right, all right,' Jake said. 'Just give me a minute . . .'

He heard the next in line tapping his foot, and closed his eyes. *Think of water. Gushing rivers. Waves. Floods.*

At last, Jake managed to go, half-filling the plastic cup. Then he flushed and turned to the basin where he washed his hands.

Outside the toilet, he passed another athlete – a long-distance runner called Matt – who was waiting with a cup in his hand.

Dr Chow was sitting at the desk in her office, scribbling something in a file.

'Erm . . . where do you want this?' Jake asked, feeling a bit weird presenting another person with a pot of his urine.

Dr Chow looked up for the briefest of moments and pointed to a tray on one of the counters. 'Over there with the others,' she said. 'Then hop up on the examination table.'

Jake did as she said. 'Is this really necessary? I mean, every day?'

'I'm afraid so,' said the doctor, still scribbling. 'If we're to establish the progress levels, then we need to know exactly what you guys are putting into your bodies. No unapproved beverages, no supplements, no drugs. Not even paracetamol, got it?'

Jake nodded, even though the doctor wasn't looking at him. 'I read the brochure.'

'Make a fist,' she said, brandishing a syringe. He did as she asked, and she slid the needle into the bulging vein in the crook of his arm. It didn't hurt a bit. He smiled to himself when he thought of how afraid his dad was of needles. He used to hate away matches in exotic locations.

'Something funny?' the doctor asked, as she drew blood into the syringe.

'Just thinking about my dad,' he said.

Dr Chow gave him a cotton ball to stem the blood, and dropped the syringe into a transparent bag. 'Your father was a famous soccer player, wasn't he?' she asked.

'He was,' Jake said. 'But he was a defender.'

'And you're not?'

'I'm a striker,' Jake said. 'Completely different.'

Dr Chow nodded, but didn't look interested any more. 'Can you take your top off, please?'

Jake pulled his T-shirt over his head, feeling the cool air on his skin.

'Hmm,' the doctor said, placing a stethoscope to his chest. 'Very good. Your resting heartbeat's about sixty a minute.'

A mobile phone rang across the room, and Dr Chow walked over to pick it up.

Jake had been at the medical centre for nearly an hour now, answering questions and having tests run. Fat ratios, grip tests, lung capacity, flexibility, vision. It all seemed a bit over the top, but Dr Chow had assured him it was all necessary. Jake just wanted to get out and kick a football around in the Florida sun.

Over in the corner of the room, a fridge hummed. Through the glass panel, he saw it was filled with bottles of Olympic Edge. In Bruce Krantz's introductory speech, he'd been clear that part of the testing was to ascertain if the drink had any physiological benefits. That was the price of sponsorship, Jake supposed.

Dr Chow giggled, and Jake tried not to listen to her conversation '. . . I can't . . . Not now, sweetie . . .' She smiled as her eyes caught Jake's. '. . . I can't *wait* . . .'

The doctor blew a kiss down the phone and hung up. Jake tried not to show his irritation at being held in this clinic while she acted like a sappy schoolgirl.

'Sorry about the interruption,' she said, suddenly businesslike again. She scribbled a few notes on a pad, and told Jake he could put his top back on. 'You're in exceptional shape.'

Jake thought straight away of Otto Kahn. He'd seemed fine – until he'd dropped dead.

'Dr Chow,' he said, hopping off the bed, 'what do you think happened to Otto?'

Dr Chow looked up from her pad with an expression of concern. 'It could be any number of things,' she said. 'Maybe the climate . . . Maybe he had a hidden heart difficulty. It sometimes happens in those who show unusual growth. But it might just have been an accident. The autopsy should tell us more.'

She opened the fridge, and offered Jake a bottle of Olympic Edge. It was the green version – 'Evolution'. He shook his head. 'I don't like the taste.'

'Take it anyway,' she said. 'It's much better than water for hydration.'

Jake took it, but dropped it in the first bin he passed as he exited the medical centre. *I'll stick with water*, he thought.

Jake was heading to the dormitories when he heard a noise he'd recognise anywhere. Leather on leather. *Football*.

He followed the sounds and came out at the artificial hockey pitch. A dozen or so guys were knocking a ball among themselves on the AstroTurf. One guy stood in the hockey goal, playing keeper.

There were several footballers at the camp, but Jake hadn't had time to meet any yet. It would be good to check out the competition. He pushed open the gate and jogged towards the group.

One of the highlights of the camp was a game at the end of the fortnight. The footballers would play a full ninety-minute friendly against the US soccer team. There were twenty potentials at the camp – a good size for a squad but, of course, there were just eleven starting places. Competition would be fierce – especially since the audience would be filled with scouts from some of the world's biggest clubs.

'Over here!' he called, holding up his arm. The guy with the ball looked up, and directed a pass along the ground to Jake.

Another player intercepted the ball with his foot when it was halfway. He flicked it into his arms. Jake recognised him from the Australian under-19 squad who'd got to the semis in the World Cup the year before: Oz Ellman.

'Sorry, but we were just leaving,' Oz said. 'Weren't we, fellas?'

The others grunted in the affirmative. Jake shrugged. 'No worries. But give me a call next time. I'm dying for a game. I'm in room fifteen B.'

As he turned to go, he heard Oz say: 'I'm sure Baby Bastin is used to getting his own way.'

Jake stopped – his temper flared. He turned to face them. 'I'm sorry. I didn't catch that.'

Oz's face set into a sneer. 'Listen, pom, don't start throwing your weight around, expecting a free ride. We all got here on *merit*. Not because our daddies pulled strings.'

'My dad had nothing to do with it,' Jake said.

This brought a round of guffaws from a couple of the other players. Most were silent, though, all eyes on Jake.

'Yeah,' Oz said. 'You getting picked for the commercial was just a coincidence, I guess?'

Jake didn't have an answer for that. Maybe his name did

21

have something to do with it. He hadn't even wanted to be in the commercial, but there was no point saying that now.

'I could name about fifty guys who should be here instead of you,' Oz added, throwing the ball hard at Jake's chest.

Jake caught the ball. It stung his chest, but he didn't flinch. Part of him wanted to rush at Oz, fists flying, but he'd seen enough pointless fighting.

'Leave it, Oz,' said someone from the back, his voice French maybe.

Jake felt a tingle of relief – not everyone here was a git.

But Oz wasn't leaving it. He was eyeballing Jake, looking for any kind of rise. Jake wasn't going to give it to him. Instead, he dropped the football and kicked it back, over the Australian's head and into the hockey goal. As he walked away, Jake grinned to himself. He'd show Oz Ellman that he was more than just a name.

4

After a high-carb dinner in the canteen, Jake and Tan took advantage of the recreation time to get out of the complex. The whole atmosphere was tainted by Otto's death. The afternoon's festivities had been cancelled and everyone seemed to be at a loose end. Krantz reminded them of the strict curfew – if they weren't back by ten, there'd be serious trouble. They signed out at the front gates and took the exit road out into town on foot. Tan was sipping a bottle of purple Olympic Edge called 'Cloudburst' as they hit the main street of Redford.

'Why you no like this stuff?' he said. 'I think it really work.' He held out the bottle. 'Try some.'

Jake sniffed the top of the bottle, and laughed. 'And I think it's all in your head. This stuff smells like toilet cleaner.'

Palm trees lined the street, ruffled by a warm breeze even though the sun was setting. Jake had seen most of the town's main drag on the way in. It wasn't a big place, maybe three or four miles across, shunting up against the southern outskirts of Miami to the north. It had a central business district with small supermarkets and clothes shops, a hardware store and a dozen or so bars and cafés. The tallest buildings in the town were a couple of five-storey office blocks.

Jake felt Tan tap his elbow. 'Look over there,' he said, nodding towards a bar called the Thirsty Alligator. The front door was guarded by a single bouncer, and some kind of Latin jazz music spilled out on to the pavement. Through the glass frontage, Jake saw what had got Tan's attention.

Dr Chow sat at a high table, a tall bottle in front of her, leaning close in conversation with a guy wearing a red baseball cap and sunglasses.

'Must be her boyfriend,' Jake said. 'I had to listen to them flirting on the phone earlier.'

'You think he works at Olympic Advantage also?' Tan asked.

Jake shrugged. 'I haven't seen him around.'

Dr Chow stared down at the table, absently playing with her glass. If they were in a relationship, it looked as if they were having an uncomfortable discussion.

'Come on,' said Tan, 'it bad if they see us watching.'

Jake was about to go when Dr Chow jabbed her index

finger at her companion's chest. Her face was strained. The man waved a finger back as if telling her she'd said something incorrect.

'Wait a second,' Jake said.

Next Dr Chow tried to lean back, only for the guy to lunge across and grip her elbow. Her face creased, registering pain.

'We need to go in,' Jake said.

'Rescuing the lady not work well before, remember?' Tan said.

Jake's eyes were on the arguing couple. Dr Chow was trying to pull away, but the guy in the cap wasn't letting go.

'Keep the bouncer busy,' Jake said.

'How?' Tan asked.

Jake nodded to the bottle in Tan's hand. 'A little spillage should do the trick.'

They waited for a gap in the traffic and crossed the street. Jake let Tan go on ahead. As his friend got to the front of the Thirsty Alligator, he pretended to trip, up-ending the bottle all over the bouncer's shoes.

'What the . . .!' the bouncer said, spreading his arms wide and stepping away from the door.

Jake walked towards the entrance, hearing Tan say: 'I'm really sorry. So clumsy.' He was positioning himself so the bouncer turned his back to Jake. Jake slipped into the bar.

The music was pretty loud inside, but he headed straight over to Dr Chow's table, weaving past a waitress. She'd finally jerked her arm free, and Jake caught the words, 'Leave me *alone*!'

'Is there a problem?' Jake asked as he reached her side.

The guy with the beer looked him up and down in less than a second, then pulled his cap lower. 'Beat it, kid.'

'Are you OK?' Jake asked Dr Chow.

'I'm fine,' she said, clearly startled. 'You shouldn't be in here, Jake.'

'Yeah, mind your own business,' said the guy. He was still trying to hide his face.

'I was just passing,' Jake said. 'I saw −'

'You saw jack,' the guy said. 'Now get lost.' He nudged him with his elbow as if trying to help him move along. Jake brushed it aside, and the guy's hand clattered into his bottle, sending beer gushing on to his lap.

'Why you little −'

'You,' said a deep voice behind him, 'show me some ID.'

A second bouncer loomed over Jake. He had the build of someone who wasn't used to arguing.

'Does he *look* old enough to have ID?' said Dr Chow's companion sarcastically, wiping at his jeans with a napkin.

The bouncer stuck a thumb towards the door. 'Out you go, before I call the cops.'

Jake hesitated for another couple of seconds, weighing his options. Should he take Dr Chow with him?

'You deaf, kid?' said the bouncer. A few people at a nearby table had turned to watch too.

Jake sighed and backed away from the couple. The guy in the cap was pointedly staring the other way. He'd never got a good look at the man's face.

The bouncer escorted him all the way to the door. Outside, Tan was still protesting his innocence, trying to wipe the bouncer's wet shoes. The bouncer, annoyed, gave Tan a light shove in the chest.

Jake's roommate stumbled back, and seemed to trip over his own feet, landing hard on the pavement. Jake thought at first Tan was just acting clumsy, but then he saw the grimace contorting his face. Jake knew real pain when he saw it. Tan stood gingerly, supporting himself against a tree trunk, favouring his right knee. He began to limp along the pavement. Jake waited until the bouncers were chatting then headed after him at a jog.

'Hey, what's up?' Jake asked.

Tan gave Jake a worried stare. He stopped again, and tried to flex his leg. 'You can keep secret?'

'Sure,' Jake replied.

Tan shook his head. 'Last year, I tear ligaments. Bad long-jump landing. I have surgery . . . But it no heal right.'

Jake frowned. 'Should you be training, then? I mean, the next couple of weeks are going to be pretty intense.'

Tan gave a thin smile. 'I guess not,' he said. 'But Olympic Advantage too good to miss, you know?'

Jake knew. It was stupid, but he understood. It would have taken a pretty serious injury to keep *him* off the plane to Miami. Tan was walking a bit smoother now, putting more weight on his leg.

'You could really hurt yourself,' Jake said.

'I take painkillers if it gets bad,' said Tan. 'And I have another operation next month. Olympic Advantage mean everything to me. Please no tell anyone.'

Tan stared hard at Jake and Jake thought of the knee injury that had ended his dad's playing career. Steve Bastin was lucky MI6 had seen his potential and recruited him. A lot of other players had ended up on the scrapheap far too early because of one mistimed tackle.

'I won't tell anyone,' Jake said. 'But be careful. Don't push yourself too hard. Don't ruin your whole future trying to prove something.'

Tan slapped Jake on the back. 'Thanks, dude. Did you

find out what problem is with jerk in bar?'

'I guess it was just a lovers' tiff,' said Jake. 'They threw me out as fast as I got in.'

Tan laughed. 'Maybe you stick to football. Stop playing hero.'

Jake raised an eyebrow. 'I think you might be right.'

The canteen was buzzing the next day at breakfast. People seemed to have forgotten all about Otto Kahn, but Jake remembered seeing him shovel down his massive breakfast just twenty-four hours before. Even Tan was back to his bouncy self.

The athletes were encouraged to log everything they ate and drank in nutrition books, so the monitors could calculate their calorie intake. Jake avoided the rainbow colours of the chilled Olympic Edge and settled for freshly squeezed orange juice.

After breakfast, he went back to the laundry to pick up his clean kit. Laundry trucks came every other day to collect the mountains of dirty gear, and deposited fresh loads at the same time. While Jake waited for his food to settle, he had a look through the local paper. There was an interview with Bruce Krantz about the previous day's tragedy, and he was already predicting the coroner would deliver a verdict of accidental death.

Jake was due to get down to the practice pitch at ten-thirty to meet the rest of the football trainees and the coach who'd guide them through the next fortnight. His name was Pedro Garcia, according to the brochure. Jake was hardly looking forward to seeing Oz Ellman again, but was excited about playing some proper football. As he laced his boots, he felt a mixture of nerves and energy. He *was* here on his own merit. 'Daddy Bastin' had nothing to do with it.

At ten-twenty, Jake jogged up to the pitch, and counted about twenty other guys standing around, all wearing the Olympic Advantage training tops with the LGE logo on the front. He thought he might be one of the youngest. There were players from all over the world, and most had formed into small groups. They stood around warming up with practice balls.

Oz's group was at the back, tapping a ball back and forth. When Oz saw Jake, he sneered, but didn't say anything.

Fine, thought Jake. *We'll soon see how good you are.*

Jake joined a group of South Americans, playing headers and volleys. That's what he loved about football – spoken language was irrelevant.

After they'd been going for a minute or so without losing the rhythm, one of the guys plucked the ball out of the air, and whispered, 'Coach is here.'

A golf-cart approached, driven by a man in a white tracksuit, with the initials 'PG' stamped over the breast. He stepped off, flanked by an assistant with a clipboard.

'Hey, fellas,' the coach said. 'Hope you're all ready for some serious training!'

When Jake heard the coach's voice, his stomach sank. Even without the red baseball cap and the bad attitude, there was no mistaking the voice.

The football coach – Pedro Garcia – was the man from the bar.

5

Garcia stood with his feet planted apart. Jake stood behind one of the guys he'd been warming up with, trying to draw as little attention to himself as possible.

'I guess Bruce has welcomed you already to Olympic Advantage,' the coach said. 'My name is Pedro Garcia.'

The player beside Jake, a Peruvian called Manny, leant closer, whispering: 'Garcia was with Corinthians in the nineties. He played for Argentina under-twenty-ones.'

Jake had trouble picturing this bulky coach doing much good on the pitch. 'What happened to him?' he asked.

The South American shrugged. 'Some cartilage problem, I think, in his feet.'

Garcia continued: 'My role at the camp is to assess every aspect of your game: speed, agility, stamina, coordination. We'll analyse tackling, dribbling, heading, jumping, set-pieces. We'll assess tactics and spatial awareness.'

Yeah, but will we play any football? Jake wondered.

'First, roll call,' said Garcia. 'Jerry here is my assistant.'

The guy with the clipboard stepped forwards and began reading names off the list. The participants called back 'here'. When he called 'Jake Bastin', and Jake shouted 'Here', Jerry paused to peer up from the clipboard. Oz sniggered something about 'not for long'.

Garcia's eyes found him now, and his face barely gave anything away: just a slight twist of the lips as if he'd tasted something rotten. The roll call continued. Jake held the coach's stare.

After roll call, they were told to break into five groups of four for relay sprints across the pitch. Jake was teamed with Manny, and two other guys called Seb and Rafe. At the whistle, Seb set off first, tagging Manny at the far side. Jake jumped on the spot, keeping himself warm. His team was actually in the lead, and he noticed Oz standing next to him, ready to go. *Time to show him I've got every right to be here.*

Manny arrived at the same time as Oz's team-mate, and Jake sprinted off, pumping his arms for extra speed as he crossed the pitch. He felt himself pulling away from the Australian, and he reached Rafe a good two metres ahead of him. Oz was puffing, hands on his knees, while Jake watched Rafe take the final leg of the relay and reach the other side first. Seb was whooping, 'We won!' and at the other side Manny and Rafe were slapping each other on the back.

Oz couldn't even look him in the eye. And didn't *that* feel good!

Coach Garcia blew his whistle. 'Sorry, guys,' he said, pointing to Jake's group, 'I'm afraid you're disqualified.'

'What?' Rafe shouted. 'Why?'

Garcia nodded at Jake. 'Jerry tells me that Bastin here was already over the line before his guy tagged him.'

'That's rubbish,' Jake said. 'No way!'

Garcia's face went darker. 'There's no place for cheating at Olympic Advantage, Jake,' he said.

Jake's blood was boiling. He hadn't been over the line – he was damn sure. He bit his tongue as Oz's team was pronounced the winner.

'Right, let's do some push-ups,' said Garcia. 'Start with fifty.'

There was a bit of groaning, but Jake got down quick. He could do fifty in his sleep. Jake counted them off, letting his anger fuel his arms. Garcia was going around, uttering words of encouragement. At twenty, Jake saw the coach's feet near his head.

'Proper push-ups, Jake,' he said. 'Nice and low. There's no prize for taking it easy.'

'I'm doing proper ones,' Jake said through gritted teeth.

He felt Garcia's hand on the small of his back. 'Keep your back straight,' he said. To others it might have appeared as if he was helping, but Jake could feel the coach pushing down, adding extra resistance. Jake knew he was being tested – or punished.

Some of the guys stopped at thirty, others collapsed around forty, but Jake kept going with half a dozen others. With the extra weight on his back, his arms were burning, and sweat dripped from his head. When he got to fifty, he sank on to the turf.

'That's good,' the coach said. 'But, Jake, you need to give us another twenty. Some of those only counted as a half.'

'You've got to be kidding,' Jake mumbled.

Coach Garcia barked a laugh. 'It's a bit early to be giving me attitude.'

'I'm not the one with the attitude,' Jake hissed.

Oz 'oohed' theatrically, drawing a sharp glare from the coach.

'Let's get one thing straight, Bastin,' Garcia said. '*I'm* the boss around here. Got it?'

Jake was about to say that Garcia liked picking on people weaker than him, but he managed to catch himself. It wouldn't do any good to make an enemy of the coach. He could make the next fortnight hell for Jake if he wanted to.

'I got it,' said Jake, readying for twenty more push-ups.

After push-ups came sit-ups, then squats and burpees. Jake was beginning to wonder if they'd actually get around to some football when Garcia called a break. Another golf cart pulled up. A guy in a pale blue suit stepped off, opening a hamper on the back of the cart. It was a cool-box, and inside were bottles of Olympic Edge.

'Drink up,' the guy said, handing out bottles and tossing one to Jake. 'It'll help keep the fires burning.' He didn't look like a trainer, and as the other players stood around, or sat on the grass drinking, he spoke quickly with a salesman's patter. 'Nothing like Olympic Edge to make you the best you can be. Just watch, in six months' time everyone will be hollering for this stuff.'

Jake unscrewed the cap, and pretended to take a sip. Even the smell of it nauseated him. He made sure no one was watching, and tipped the drink away on to a dry patch of ground.

'My name's Phillips,' the suited man said. 'Edgar Phillips. Marketing director for LGE. Fuelling the future of sport.'

The slogan was almost as sickening to Jake as their product – which everyone else seemed to be really enjoying.

'I'm not just here as the waterboy,' Phillips said. 'I've come to give you guys the lowdown on our fast-track scheme. LGE needs a few select athletes to serve as brand ambassadors –' he used air quotes around the term – 'to represent LGE to the wider world.' Everyone was listening intently. 'And you wouldn't be working for free, of course,' Phillips continued. 'We have a number of grants – substantial grants, I might add – to fund the chosen faces. LGE can help with training expenses, equipment, access to facilities – you name it – for the lucky ones. We'll make sure you have everything you need.'

Some of the other athletes were nodding excitedly, and even Jake found he was interested now. Was there a chance this guy could help him turn pro? It seemed too good to be true.

'How much are the grants?' Oz asked.

'How much do you want?' the marketing man replied. 'The sky's the limit, really. LGE will pay big bucks for the right person.' He grinned again. Jake found it off-putting, and Phillips's too-white teeth shook him out of his reverie. *Like a shark before he bites.* There was something slimy about him, the way his eyes shifted from one athlete to the next, as if weighing up their worth to the 'brand'. Jake didn't trust him. Not one bit.

Jake decided he was only here to play football.

After the break, Garcia finally divided them into two groups for a practice match. There were no goalkeepers on the camp – not as much marketing potential, Jake supposed – so the coach picked a couple of players to stand between the sticks. Jake half-expected to get chosen through sheer spite, but it was Rafe and a young Saudi called Jamal.

Everyone seemed a little tense, Jake included. The stuff up till now had been the preliminaries. This was the real deal, the chance to impress. And, of course, the possibility of being picked for the big match against the US team.

Jake was glad of his shin pads. Five minutes in, and he was being kicked about every time he got the ball. Garcia was refereeing, and Jake was pretty sure the coach would only blow his whistle if someone punched Jake in the face. Maybe not even then. Oz and his goons were the worst, but even some of the others, guys Jake had thought friendly, seemed to want to get a few kicks in too.

But it wasn't just Jake – players all over the pitch were getting clattered. Seb and an Ivorian player, Benoit, got into a pushing match on the halfway line.

'Take it easy!' shouted Garcia. 'We want to get to the end of camp without any injuries.'

Jake picked up a pass near the halfway line, taking the ball away from another midfielder. He exchanged a one-two with

Seb, who was tight on the wing, and got the ball back thirty metres out. Taking in the field with a sweep of his eyes, he saw a Spanish player called Miguel making a run from midfield, screaming for the pass, but Jake had space. He brought the ball on to his favoured right foot, a couple of metres nearer, and eyed the top corner of the goal. It was ambitious, but nothing ventured . . .

Jake swung his foot through the ball, giving it some inward spin. A normal-sized keeper would have struggled to get across in time. Jamal had no chance. Jake waited to see the net balloon, but suddenly his legs went from underneath him, and he hit the ground, completely winded.

The rest of the team were cheering the goal. Jake rolled over, trying to get his breath, and saw a pair of distinctive silver boots. Oz Ellman.

'Watch it!' said Jake.

Oz spat on to the turf – centimetres from Jake's face. 'If you can't hack *real* football, then have a kickabout in your backyard with Daddy.'

It took everything Jake had not to act out the scene in his head – him jumping up and slamming a straight right into Oz's jaw. But the loudmouth Australian was already jogging over to his cronies. Garcia, who was doing a good impression of a blind referee, not having seen Oz's red-card-worthy challenge, gestured for the game to continue. Jake was annoyed when he failed to control a long looping pass on his chest. It bounced to Tanaka, a Japanese player, who stroked a through ball up to Oz. Jake couldn't deny Oz was skilled. He outwitted the first defender with a neat stepover, then charged the box. Jake sprinted after him. Oz went round another defender, but the ball got caught up between his feet. It gave Jake time to draw level. As the Australian was righting himself, Jake went in shoulder first, sending him tumbling. It was a fair challenge.

Well, borderline.

Oz was up in a flash, and Jake knew what was coming. When Oz shoved him hard with both hands in the chest, Jake braced himself and shoved back, getting a handful of Oz's collar.

Oz slipped a foot behind Jake's and they overbalanced, toppling on to the grass. He heard the whistle going, and realised others were running in, but Jake just wanted to get the upper hand. Oz drove a fist into his ribs. Jake barely felt it. His blood was pounding.

'That's *enough*!' shouted Garcia. Jake felt himself yanked off Oz and dragged back out of the way. Oz, flushed in the face, was straightening his jersey where it had torn at the collar.

'You two are an absolute disgrace!' Garcia shouted. 'Get off my field this minute!'

Jake knew there was no point arguing with the coach; he'd let himself down. Shame flooded into his veins, quenching the rush of adrenalin and anger. Dropping his head, he walked off the pitch.

Oz stomped to the sidelines as well, a few metres away from Jake.

'This ain't over,' Oz muttered.

Jake showered, and was throwing on a shirt as the other guys finished up on the pitch. He didn't feel like talking, so took the path towards the stadium, hoping to catch Tan practising his events.

'Hey, Jake,' someone called out. Garcia.

Jake kept walking, pretending not to hear.

'Bastin, I'm talking to you.'

Jake stopped. *Here comes another lecture.*

The coach jogged up to him.

'Jake, what happened out there today was unacceptable. The whole ethos of Olympic Advantage is teamwork – helping your fellow athletes raise their game.'

Jake wanted to tell Garcia all about Oz constantly needling him, but what was the point? You had to handle some problems yourself.

'I'm informing the camp director,' Garcia continued.

'Bet you'll just love that . . .' Jake muttered.

Garcia straightened, his eyes widening a fraction. 'What did you say, you little jerk? You're going to have to keep yourself in check, you hear me?'

'Guess I'm not the only one with a temper.' The words were out of Jake's mouth before he could stop them.

Garcia shot a shifty glance both ways. They were hidden by a small equipment shed. Out of sight. The coach stepped forwards until his face was less than a foot from Jake's. They were about the same height, and Jake stared him in the eye.

'Be careful, kid,' Garcia said. 'One word from me, and you won't just be heading to the locker room. You'll be on the first flight home.'

'I'm bigger than Dr Chow,' Jake said. 'Not as easy to push around.' He shouldn't have said it, but he hated a bully.

'You mind your own business,' Garcia said, stabbing Jake in the chest with a finger. 'When I push, it's not pretty.'

As the coach turned to walk away, Jake thought he saw a flash of Oz's blond hair through the bushes.

Maybe they weren't alone after all.

6

'How was your morning?' Tan asked, taking a bread roll from the basket.

Jake was behind him in the canteen queue. He wasn't all that hungry, but they'd been told to load up on carbs before the afternoon's training sessions, so his tray was full. He helped himself to a couple of bananas.

'It was fine,' Jake said. No need to burden Tan with his troubles.

Tan took a couple of bottles of blue Olympic Edge from the chill cabinet. He held one up. 'I score personal best in javelin this morning.'

'Sounds like you're buying the hype,' Jake laughed, as he took a bottle of water.

'No, I am serious,' Tan said.

'And how's your knee?' Jake whispered as they placed their trays on an empty table.

Tan's head snapped up, his eyes panicked. 'I tell you not to mention it!' he hissed.

Jake, slightly taken aback, looked around. 'No one heard. Chill out. I was only asking.'

'Well, please do not,' Tan mumbled.

They ate in silence. Jake fished around in his head for something to say. With all the enemies he was making, he needed as many friends as possible at the camp. He was about to ask Tan about the standard of the other decathletes when Veronika came into the canteen with Maria, another tennis player. They were wearing tennis whites – with the LGE logo, of course – and carrying large racket bags over their shoulders. Jake felt his eyebrows rise – if Veronika had been playing all morning in the thirty-degree heat, she looked very good for it. Her skin was the colour of honey, and her long hair was tied in a ponytail hanging over her shoulder.

When she saw Jake, she gave him a little wave. Her companion whispered something. Jake guessed whatever it was couldn't have been too bad, because Veronika whispered back.

Perhaps he'd done *something* right . . .

'Hey!' someone shouted. 'Back off and wait your turn!'

All heads turned to the canteen queue. Two girls were shoving each other. Carolina Tuletti, the Italian synchronised swimmer, smashed a loaded tray from the hands of Su-Lin, a Chinese table-tennis player. Su-Lin responded by grabbing a fistful of Carolina's hair and yanking her head down. Carolina's hands formed a claw that raked at Su-Lin's face.

Everyone was watching, dumbfounded, until Jake sprang up to put his body between the two screaming girls. An elbow came out of nowhere, connecting with the point of Jake's jaw, and making his head spin. He managed to get his arms around Su-Lin and, with others helping or getting in between, they pulled the kicking, spitting girls apart. Su-Lin struggled against him. 'Let me go! Let me at her!'

Another short fuse, Jake thought. Clearly the spirit of competition was alive and well at Olympic Advantage.

'We leave?' Tan said, finishing his bottle of Riptide. 'Very embarrassing if we get knocked out by *synchronised swimmer*!'

When he was sure that Su-Lin had calmed down, Jake released her.

'Let's go,' he said, flexing his jaw.

Jake checked one of the timetables posted up around the complex and saw that there was a two-hour optional session after lunch. He had to read it twice to make sure he'd got it right.

'Are you serious . . . *Yoga*?'

Tan laughed. 'Good for tone.'

'I'd rather go for a run,' Jake said. After the morning's aborted training session, he felt he needed to burn off some energy.

They took a path back to the dorms, passing a couple of stocky guys who could have been twins. Both wore judo suits. The track ran up alongside a wooden fence two and a half metres high.

'I wonder what's over other side,' Tan said.

'Let's take a peek.' Jake jumped, reaching for the top, and pulled himself up to look over. He saw a field littered with archery targets. Young men and women with state-of-the-art composite bows were bracing themselves to shoot.

Tan heaved himself up beside Jake. Beyond was the rowing lake, set up with boathouses around the outside.

'This place must cost much dollar,' Tan said.

'And all paid for by LGE,' Jake replied, lowering himself back down. 'No wonder Phillips wants to get the most out of us.'

They continued down the path, pausing at the gymnastic hall's glass viewing panel. Jake marvelled at the tumbling athletes. One girl, with her perfectly executed flips, reminded him of a girl he'd met in Milan – Abri Kuertzen, the supermodel.

Well, supermodel-slash-diamond thief.

When they arrived at their dorm block, Jake punched the

entrance code, and led the way back along the corridor to 15B, their room on the ground floor. Security was obviously a prime concern at Olympic Advantage. Most doors were only accessible if you had the right code. There were security men and women scattered throughout the facilities, all dressed in a casual uniform of khakis and polo shirts, but still carrying handguns on their hips, as well as mace and tasers. Jake thought it was a bit over the top.

As they said polite hellos to the baseball player and sprinter who shared room 12, Jake took the key-card out of his pocket. It served as his ID, with his photo and details, but was also programmed to give him access to certain parts of the facility and, specifically, the room he shared with Tan. He was about to run it through the reader by the door handle when he saw that the door was already open. Just an inch . . .

'That's weird,' he whispered. 'Have you been back since this morning?'

Tan shook his head. 'We call security?'

'I can handle it,' Jake said. He felt a prickle of fear along his spine, but shoved the door open. It clattered against the adjacent wall. There was no one inside.

But there had been.

'Oh, no!' Tan gasped.

Both beds had been tossed. The mattresses were on the

floor, the sheets and pillows scattered. The wardrobe doors had been opened and the contents were strewn across the room. Tan immediately went to his bedside drawer where he kept his valuables. He sighed with relief.

'My passport and money still here,' he said.

Jake checked his. Same story.

'Someone playing trick,' Tan said grimly.

Jake nodded. One name sprung to mind: Oz.

But why bring Tan into this as well? That seemed petty, even for an idiot like Oz. And it didn't explain how someone had been able to enter in the first place. Jake was one hundred per cent sure he'd closed the door that morning.

Someone must have been *looking* for something.

Had they found it?

An hour later, Jake signed out at the front gate and set off at a slow jog towards the town. Tan had opted for the yoga, but Jake needed time to think about the situation with Coach Garcia. On the one hand, he wanted to succeed at Olympic Advantage, but there was no way he was going to get selected by the coach if they were at loggerheads the whole time. He wondered if he needed to swallow his pride, live with the hypocrisy, and just apologise.

The sun was beating down as Jake reached the main

street. He felt good. Running often got his thoughts in order. He passed a second-hand car dealership, and then the bar where he'd seen Garcia pestering Dr Chow. Maybe the coach was right. It wasn't any of Jake's business. They were just having an argument, like any couple.

Jake knew a thing or two about couples arguing. He'd been eight when his parents split, but the preceding months had been awful. Raised voices, slammed doors.

And one day, Jake came downstairs to find his dad's car was gone . . .

Jake ran past a swanky café with tables arranged on a terrace out front. There weren't many customers at that time of day, and one in particular caught Jake's attention. He stopped suddenly.

The guy was sitting, sprawled on a chair, a half-finished cup of coffee on the table in front of him. His face was obscured by a newspaper, but Jake wasn't looking at his face. He was staring at the man's shoes. Scruffy Nikes, at least a year past their best. Most people would have been embarrassed to leave the house in them. But someone Jake knew very well insisted they were the most comfortable shoes he'd ever owned.

'Dad?' Jake said.

The paper dropped, and there sat Steve Bastin. Tanned and relaxed.

'Hi, Jake,' he said. 'What are you doing here?'

'What are *you* doing here?' Jake countered. 'You said you'd keep your distance. You said you'd be up in Miami!'

'I'm just having a drink with some old friends,' his dad said with an innocent shrug.

A beautiful blonde woman slinked out of the café, giving Jake a strange look as she took the seat beside his dad.

'Anna,' Jake's dad said, 'meet my son, Jake.'

The blonde held out a manicured hand and Jake took it in a limp handshake.

'Old friends?' Jake asked his dad.

'Well, my other friends haven't arrived yet,' he said. 'They're involved with the Olympic Advantage camp.'

Huh? His dad had never mentioned having friends at the camp.

The sweat was cooling on Jake's skin. There was no need to get angry – his dad had every right to sit wherever he wanted, with whomever he wanted. But his dad seemed to be lying again . . .

'Can I have a word, Dad?' he said. He frowned at Anna. 'In private.'

'Sure,' said his dad, standing up and walking with Jake under the shade of a palm tree. 'What is it?'

'Dad, you remember when I was first approached for the

camp, back in Milan?' His dad nodded. 'Well, I just wanted to ask: did you have anything to do with it? Pull any strings?'

His dad shook his head, but looked Jake in the eye. 'Nothing at all, Jake.'

'You promise?'

'I swear on my FA Cup Winner's Medal,' his dad said. 'You're here on your own merit.'

Jake felt in his gut that his dad was telling the truth. Since he'd found out about his dad's secret life as an MI6 spy, Jake had got pretty good at telling when he was lying. He smiled, and nodded over his dad's shoulder. 'I'll let you get back to your "coffee".'

His dad slapped him on the back, wished him good luck at the camp and Jake continued on his run, feeling a fresh sense of determination. He deserved to be here.

Now he just had to prove it to the others.

When Jake arrived back at the camp, the security guys seemed more uptight than usual. He was held at the gate while a phone call was made.

'What's the matter?' Jake asked one of the female guards.

'We're finding that out,' she replied.

A few minutes later, one of the complex buggies pulled up. Bruce Krantz stepped out, and beckoned Jake over.

Much to Jake's annoyance, two security guards flanked him all the way.

'What's going on?' Jake asked. 'Why am I being treated like a criminal?'

Krantz's face was grave. 'Where have you been?'

'Out for a run,' Jake said. 'No law against that, is there?'

'Less lip,' said one of the guards, bristling.

The director put up a hand to calm him down. 'Have you seen Coach Garcia?'

'Not since practice this morning,' Jake said. 'What's all this about?'

'It might be nothing,' Krantz said, though his face suggested anything but. 'We're struggling to get hold of him. He normally answers his phone straight away.'

'Yeah, so?' Jake shrugged.

'You had an altercation with Coach Garcia earlier, didn't you?' the guard asked.

'Tempers flared on the pitch, that's all. That happens in football,' Jake said.

The guard's eyes narrowed. 'I'm not talking about the practice. Afterwards, you two were seen arguing.'

Damn Oz! He must have told security.

'That was just a chat,' Jake said. 'He was telling me how I could lose my marker in the box. I'm sure he'll show up.'

'Fine, fine,' Krantz said. 'There won't be any official practice this afternoon, though. We've lined up some circuits for you guys. Good to see you're getting some exercise anyway.'

As Jake walked back to his room, he felt a ball of worry building in his stomach. If Oz had told security, he'd have told everyone else as well. Jake could handle one or two people turning against him, but not the whole squad. And with Otto's death, and whoever had trashed their room, this fortnight in the sunshine was turning pretty dark. Jake wasn't sure yet, but he was beginning to think that there might be something nasty going on at Olympic Advantage.

He hoped Garcia showed up soon.

7

Jake woke early the next morning, feeling jumpy about the day ahead. He'd spent the evening before watching a fencing competition and trying clear his mind, but it hadn't worked. Plus he felt bad about lying to Dr Chow. During the daily tests with her, she'd asked how much of the Olympic Edge he was consuming, and he'd been honest, saying that he didn't like it. She'd suggested one of the other flavours available, so Jake had said he'd give it a try. That 'try' had consisted of sniffing one of the other bottles and then pouring it down the sink.

Tan was buzzing at breakfast. He said he'd now set personal records in nine of his ten events, and beat his hundred-metre PB by half a second. Olympic Advantage was bringing out the best in Tan. Maybe there was something to that horrible drink.

All I want is one good clean game without all the animosity, never mind setting records, Jake thought.

Jake couldn't find his kit bag afterwards, even though he

was sure he'd left it near the entrance to the canteen. Tan helped him look for it, talking the whole time, and they found it on the opposite side of the canteen under one of the tables. It seemed a petty prank, even for Oz.

So Jake ended up being five minutes late for practice. All the players were in a huddle as he sprinted to join them. He guessed that Coach Garcia had shown up after all. He dreaded the lecture that was sure to come . . . Coach Garcia didn't need another reason to dislike him.

Today, Jake promised himself, *there'll be no talking back, and I'll control my temper whatever the provocation. I am going to give it all, be a model player.*

As the huddle broke, Jake skidded to a halt. It wasn't Pedro Garcia in the middle.

It was his father.

'OK, boys, just a bit of light jogging to warm up,' he shouted. 'Twice round the pitch.'

Jake was speechless. As the players streamed past, Oz leant in close.

'What a *surprise*!' he said. 'Now we know how you got a place – your dad offered his services. You must be really proud, Baby Bastin.'

When the others were finally out of earshot, Jake rounded on his dad.

'What the hell are you doing here, Dad?'

'Look, Jake, I can explain –'

'Just for once I'd like to be something other than the great Steve Bastin's son!'

Jake's dad lifted his palms. 'Listen, I met up with Bruce Krantz yesterday. He is the old friend I was talking about. It was supposed to just be a catch-up, but he called this morning and asked me to step in as coach.'

'Just like that?' Jake asked sarcastically.

'I promise,' his dad said. 'If I hadn't accepted, they'd have had to cancel the football part of the programme. You'd all have been sent home. Jake, I only did it because I know how much this means to you.'

'But . . .' Jake began, but what did it matter if his dad was telling the truth? All the taunts, the sly digs, the insinuations of nepotism . . . they were about to get a hundred times worse.

'You'd better warm up too,' his dad said. 'Otherwise, I'm going to get accused of favouritism.'

Jake turned and sprinted to catch up with others. 'You don't know the half of it,' he muttered.

Jake tried to concentrate on his game, not the new coach. They split into different teams from the day before, so Oz and Jake were actually partnered up front. Problem was they weren't exactly on the same wavelength in a Gerrard-and-Torres style. They made the same off-the-ball runs, chased the same through passes, and twice collided mid-air trying to head the ball goalwards. The second time, as he lay on the ground after a clash of heads, Oz offered a hand to help him up. Jake took it, only to feel Oz's fingernails dig into the back of his hand, nearly drawing blood.

But it wasn't only Oz. Jake felt the whole squad was frustrated and angry. There were dangerous high tackles flying all over the field, and sliding challenges with studs raised. However much his dad blew the whistle, or cautioned players to be less aggressive, it didn't seem to calm them down. Jake got several elbows in the ribs during set pieces, and another player's shirt was torn when he was down. The player who'd raked him with studs claimed it was an accident, but from Jake's angle, seeing the guy's angry face, it had looked deliberate.

By half-time, several players were limping. The score was 3–0 to the opposition and the rest of Jake's team were getting fed up.

'Come on, Jake,' Manny said. 'Can't you work harder? We're getting embarrassed out there.'

'Strikers are all the same,' said another. 'Only interested in themselves.'

Oz pushed Manny out of the way. 'If you guys could string two passes together, we might get back into it. Anyway, Bastin needn't worry. He could play like a drunk and he'll still get picked for the big game.'

'No doubt,' Rafe said. 'Must be good to have your dad on the selectors' committee.'

Jake let it pass, but inside he was more upset than angry. Rafe had been his mate the day before, but now he seemed to be siding with the pack. Jake managed to get a single goal in the second half, but so did the other team. It finished 4−1 at the final whistle, and Jake was glad to get off the pitch without getting seriously hurt.

The afternoon session was no better. More of the same. Tempers flaring. Eleven players all competing against each other as well as the opposite team. They were all battered and bruised after the 'friendly' game. Afterwards he walked off his stiffness by heading over to the tennis courts. He spotted Veronika's blonde hair from a hundred metres off. She and her friend from the canteen were on the grass courts, practising their serves from opposite ends.

Jake, who was a pretty keen player himself, saw straight away that he wouldn't stand a chance against athletes of this calibre. Veronika's first serve was ferocious. The electronic speedometer at the side of the court didn't dip below ninety miles per hour. Watching from the edge of the court, the ball was a blur. Facing it head-on, Jake wondered if he'd see it at all.

Veronika's coach – whom Jake recognised as a Wimbledon runner-up from the seventies, Sven Arjensen – called out encouragement to her each time the ball went in, which it did eight times out of ten.

Jake had just got settled on a grass bank when the session ended. Veronika stowed her racket and took a long drink of Olympic Edge Magma. She noticed Jake, and then her eyes flicked off to the left. He tracked her line of sight and saw the same dark 4x4 parked at the top of the verge. If there was anyone inside, the tinted windows were hiding them.

He expected Veronika to walk the other way, but instead she came through the wire-mesh wall that surrounded the court and straight up the bank towards him.

'You want to get out of here for a while?' she said casually.

'Er, sure,' Jake said, wondering if this was the same girl who'd told him to keep his distance previously.

Veronika's eyes flitted to the 4x4 again.

'Come on, then,' she said quickly. 'My car's down near the administration buildings.'

'You have a car, *here*?' He suddenly felt embarrassed – he

wasn't even old enough to drive in the UK, but, of course, Americans could learn at sixteen.

'It's nothing special,' she said.

They walked towards the front gates where the main offices were. Jake offered to carry her racket bag, but she said no and picked up her pace. She seemed to want to get away as soon as possible.

'Who are those guys in the car?' Jake asked.

'Just some rich fans.' Veronika laughed, but it was hollow.

'What, like stalkers?' Jake said. 'You should tell Mr Krantz. Security will get rid of them.'

'It's nothing I can't handle,' Veronika said.

Jake knew she was hiding something, but he didn't push it.

At the car park, Veronika pulled out a set of keys. A beep sounded and the brake lights on an ice–blue metallic Porsche Boxster flashed for a second.

'Nothing special, huh?' Jake said, as she popped the boot and placed the bag inside.

She gave a casual shrug. 'One of the better things about my dad, I guess. What do you drive?'

Jake blushed. 'I don't. You have to be seventeen in the UK.'

She frowned. 'How old *are* you?'

'Sixteen.'

'Funny, you seem older,' she said with a laugh.

Jake got into the car so she didn't see him blush again.

Veronika drove out of the complex and away from the town, past a second-hand car garage and out into the landscape of the Florida Everglades. As Jake watched the miles of deep green forests and swamps pass, he struggled for something to say. It was Veronika who broke the silence.

'So I heard your dad's famous. He's here, right?'

Jake could have screamed. *Can't I for one minute escape the shadow of the famous Steve Bastin?*

'Trust me,' he said, 'it was as much of a surprise to me. He stepped in as Coach Garcia's emergency replacement. It's not doing much for my cred.'

Veronika nodded. 'I know a thing or two about parental baggage.'

'Oh, yeah?' Jake said. 'But I bet your dad isn't standing on the other side of the net serving aces at you.'

Veronika laughed. 'You got me there. I don't think my dad even knows the rules of tennis. I don't see him often, and when I do it's always on his schedule.'

They drove on until they reached a signpost that read Saddleback Swamp, 200 yards. Veronika turned on to a track.

'One of the cleaning staff told me about this place,' she said. 'I've been a couple of times, when I want to be alone.'

Jake couldn't imagine someone like Veronika hanging

around with the cleaning staff. Perhaps he had her wrong, after all. They drove through a gate and into a gravel car park leading to a clutch of picnic tables. The sun was a disc of pale light just above the horizon.

There were no other cars, so Veronika parked the Porsche at a skewed angle facing the swamp. As she popped her door, a blast of warm air filled the interior. She reached behind her seat and plucked out a couple of bottles of water, handing one to Jake.

'Thanks,' he said. 'I'm glad it's not Olympic Edge.'

'You're telling me,' she replied. 'I'm fed up with that stuff. Do you think it does what they say it does?'

Jake shook his head. 'To be honest, I've not been drinking it. Tastes like crap.'

Veronika sucked in an exaggerated breath. 'Don't let Phillips find out.'

They wandered over to a picnic table. Jake was about to take a swig of his water when he saw a sign saying 'Beware Alligators'.

'You sure this place is safe?' he asked.

'Apparently they rarely come out when it's hot,' Veronika replied. 'You want one of these?' She handed Jake an energy bar as they sat side by side on the bench, watching the sun deepening to orange. Jake looked out of the corner of his eye at Veronika. Her hair was golden now, and she seemed happy to sit in silence and enjoy the view. But why had she brought him up here? A day before, he'd have been surprised to get a smile off her. The sky dissolved to grey as the sun sank out of view. The heat went out of the day quickly, and Jake felt goose bumps rise along his arms.

'So what are you going to do about your dad?' Veronika asked.

Jake sighed. 'Keep my head down, practise hard. Try not to lose my temper . . . Easier said than done.'

Veronika chewed on her energy bar and swallowed. 'My dad's got a temper too. Problem is nobody dares tell him to stay cool.'

'What does your dad do?' Jake asked.

'He's a businessman.' Veronika chuckled. 'Does what's necessary to earn the almighty buck.' She took out the final piece of the energy bar. 'Watch this.' She threw it into the swamp, a good twenty metres out. It landed with a *plop* in the murky water.

A few seconds later, movement stirred the surface. A shushing sound reached Jake's ears. 'Is that what I think it is?'

'Not scared, are you?' Veronika asked, giving him a playful nudge in the ribs.

Jake swallowed. 'I hear they always go for girls first.'

Now a large section of the swamp swirled to life. Scaled backs emerged from the water like rising submarines, and massive tails waved sinuously, driving the alligators towards the place the energy bar had landed.

'Come on, let's go,' Veronika said.

As she stood up, something rolled to the surface against one of the swamp banks. Not an alligator. Something that didn't belong.

'What's that?' he said, squinting and pointing.

'I can't see anything,' Veronika said. It was almost dark now.

'Flick the headlights on,' Jake said.

Veronika went back to the car, and did as he asked. Suddenly the swamp was illuminated in the beams. The light caught the alligators' eyes, making them look like silver coins floating just above the water.

But Jake stared at the edge of the left bank where the object had surfaced. Something like a half-submerged log rested in the shallow water. His heart was thumping and his skin felt icy cold.

Veronika walked over to him. 'What is it?'

Jake moved to stand between her and the swamp. 'Don't come any closer.'

She frowned. 'Don't be such an idiot, Jake.' She came up and peered past him. Half a second later, she screamed.

The sound pierced the night, making a couple of the alligators thrash in the water.

Jake pulled Veronika close and she folded into him, shielding her eyes from the awful sight.

The thing in the water wasn't a log. It was a body, or part of one, with a red baseball cap floating in the shallows.

'Looks like we found Coach Garcia,' Jake said.

8

The winch attached to the police pick-up made a high-pitched grinding noise that set Jake's teeth on edge. The alligators had mostly disappeared again beneath the surface, but the spotlights set up around the edge of the water showed a few watching the scene dispassionately. A couple of cops with high-powered rifles patrolled the bank, just in case any got too curious. Coach Garcia's car emerged from the water like a forgotten shipwreck, spilling water out of the broken rear windscreen.

Jake had phoned the police immediately, and they'd taken less than ten minutes to arrive at the scene. An hour and a half after the call, an unmarked sedan carrying detectives from the homicide squad in Miami had pulled up too.

Jake tore his gaze from the covered stretcher that held Garcia's body. Or what was left of it. He was missing both legs and an arm. Jake was glad it was dark. One of the cops who'd helped drag the corpse out of the water had hurled his guts up behind his squad car.

'So tell me again,' said Detective Merski. 'You guys just happened to drive to this spot?'

They were standing beside the detective's car, going over what had happened. Or their 'version', as Merski insisted on calling it.

'Someone at the camp told me about it,' Veronika explained. 'Said it was pretty up here. Rita, or Ruth, or something like that. Oh, God, I can't believe it . . .'

'Calm down, young lady,' said Merski. 'I need to get the facts straight. You and your boyfriend here were making out, you see the body –'

'Hey, we weren't *making out*,' Jake interrupted. 'We just came for a drive, that's all.'

Merski fixed him with tired eyes. One of the uniformed officers came up alongside him.

'Sir, looks like the deceased's car came off the main road. There's broken foliage and skid marks consistent with that.'

Merski sighed. 'Thanks, Harris.' He waved a hand at Jake and Veronika. 'I've got *a lot* more questions for these two lovebirds, but I'm gonna let them go for now, unless you have anything else to ask them.'

Harris stared at them. 'Cut them loose. I've spoken to

Bruce Krantz. Their story checks out so far. They are attending Krantz's camp. He said we can question them there later if need be.'

Merski left them and went to speak with the paramedics, who were loading Garcia into the back of an ambulance to ship to the morgue. Veronika was pale in the starlight.

'You OK?' Jake asked her.

She snorted. 'No. Are *you*?'

Jake didn't want to say it wasn't the first dead body he'd seen. 'Bit of a shock,' he said.

They walked past where Detective Harris was picking weeds off the dented wreck of Garcia's car. He tugged open the door on the passenger side and more swamp water poured out, splashing over his shoes. 'Damn it!' he said, before peering in. Then, 'He's been at the booze,' he continued.

He reached inside, and pulled out an almost empty bottle of Jack Daniel's. When he noticed Jake and Veronika watching, he gave them a dark stare. Jake saw there were several empty bottles of Olympic Edge in the passenger seat too.

'You two, get outta here!' Harris snapped. 'This is a crime scene, not a spectator sport.'

Jake and Veronika got into her car. She paused with the key in the ignition. 'I don't think this was an accident.'

'Me neither,' Jake replied. 'Two dead bodies in three days, both linked to Olympic Advantage.'

'You think Otto and Garcia's deaths are connected?' Veronika asked.

Jake nodded. His experiences over the last few months had taught him to question everything. They stared through the windscreen at the eerie scene. Police and alligators swarming the swamp. It didn't appear that Merski and his crew believed in deadly coincidence either. 'We can't just sit around and wait for something else to happen. What if someone else gets hurt, or worse?'

Veronika started the engine. 'We probably should leave it to the police.'

'I wouldn't trust Merski to tie his own shoelaces,' Jake quipped.

Veronika smiled, then caught herself. 'You're right. Maybe it's time to do a little investigation of our own.'

'What have Otto and Garcia got in common?' Jake asked, his detective skills already in overdrive.

'Nothing other than Olympic Advantage,' Veronika replied. 'They weren't the same nationality, the same sport, or the same age.'

'The first thing we need to do is collect the facts. What's really going on at Olympic Advantage?'

'Whatever it is, someone would kill for it,' Veronika added. 'We should divide and conquer. I can take Krantz. He's due to come by and watch the tennis tomorrow.'

'I'll speak with Phillips,' Jake said. 'I can pretend I want to know more about these branding grants. Let's meet up at the track-and-field exhibition tomorrow afternoon.' Jake paused, suddenly unsure if getting Veronika involved was such a good idea. 'If we're going to do this, we have to be careful, OK? We can't trust anyone.'

'Except each other.' Veronika turned to face Jake. 'Give me your hand.'

Jake did as she asked. She grabbed a pen from her handbag and scribbled ten digits on his palm. 'You might need this.' She closed his hand and smiled her stunning all-American-girl smile.

A day ago, Jake would have been pleased to have scored the phone number of such a beautiful girl, but under the circumstances it felt more like a business transaction. 'I'll text you so you have mine.'

'Guess we're a team now,' Veronika said, and spun the wheels as she accelerated out of the parking lot. They drove back to the complex in silence. Jake let the reality sink in. Was there really a killer on the loose at Olympic Advantage?

*

Tan was asleep when Jake finally got back to his room. Jake had a shower to get rid of the stench of death that seemed to cling to his skin. But when he crawled beneath the sheets, he couldn't sleep. Every time he shut his eyes, he saw Coach Garcia's mangled body and imagined those moments after he'd crashed into the swamp. Jake hadn't liked the guy, but he wouldn't wish that on anyone. He only hoped Garcia had been dead or unconscious before the alligators got to him.

Next morning Jake was up with the sun. His morning session was circuit training. Half the footballing group was teamed up with athletes from other disciplines, including Tan. They went through two hours of high-intensity, multiple-repetition exercises in Olympic Advantage's state-of-the-art gym studio. Their tutor was an ex-marine called Sandy, who seemed capable of only two things: shouting and blowing a whistle loudly.

The mood among the others was grim, partly because of the gruelling training, but also because the news of Garcia's death had seeped across the complex. No one seemed to know exactly what had happened, or that Jake and Veronika had been involved. That suited Jake fine.

As the marine was winding down with a few stretches, Jake saw Phillips passing the window in a golf cart. He made some excuse and left the studio. He jogged along the track searching for Phillips's buggy, but couldn't see it anywhere. He was about to turn back when he saw the cart pulled up alongside the rear wall of the medical centre.

Jake watched Phillips walk round the back of the cart and take out a full crate of Olympic Edge. Laden under the weight, he staggered out of sight again. That was weird: how come the head of marketing was acting as a delivery boy?

Jake walked over, ready to offer his help, but as he rounded the corner of the building he saw Dr Chow holding open the back door. Something about the way she was standing, nervously glancing this way and that, made Jake retreat out of sight.

What's she so worried about?

He peered round again, and saw Phillips emerge from the open door. As he did, he slid his arm behind Dr Chow's back, and they leant together, kissing each other passionately.

Jake backed off again. *Hadn't Dr Chow been seeing Pedro Garcia?* Jake wondered. If so, she was over him quicker than a common cold.

Maybe Jake had got it wrong. Maybe it wasn't Garcia on the phone that day during the physical making Dr Chow act like a teenager; maybe it had been Phillips. Garcia might have been just an unwelcome pest, trying to hit on Dr Chow when she wanted nothing to do with him. In that case, Phillips − and perhaps Dr Chow too – had a motive for wanting Garcia out of the way.

Jake waited until he heard the electric whine of the golf cart, then watched Phillips head towards the gym block. He followed at a quick walk.

The gym was all glass on one side, retractable in good weather. It was half open now, and Jake could see Oz and a few of the others side by side on the rowing machines. The fixed and free weights were at the back of the building, along with a full-size boxing ring. Phillips stopped the cart beside the building and carried in an armful of Olympic Edge bottles, passing them out to the athletes.

Jake entered the gym and got on to a cross-trainer. He was close enough to hear when Phillips's phone rang. In the reflection of the window glass, he saw the marketing man break away from the boxing ring, and lift the phone to his ear.

Jake couldn't hear much of what followed, because Phillips was speaking with his voice low, and Oz and his guys were shouting to each other as they raced on the rowers.

'I got you,' Phillips was saying. 'I'm handling it as best I can. I know we don't need any more bad publicity. What can I say? Garcia was a drunk.'

Phillips hung up as he walked out of the door. Jake climbed

off the cross-trainer and caught up with him at the cart. Oz was watching him suspiciously from the rowing machine. Probably wondering why he'd only done two minutes on the cross-trainer.

'Mr Phillips, can I have a word?' Jake asked.

Philips turned round, and found his smile in a split second. 'Hey, Jake Bastin, isn't it? Call me Ed. What can I do for you?'

'It's about the grants you were talking about,' Jake said. 'I'm interested in becoming a brand ambassador.'

Phillips raised an eyebrow. 'I'm sure you are, young man,' he said, 'and I'm sure LGE would be interested in being associated with someone of your –' *name*, Jake thought – 'calibre,' Philips continued, 'but there are official channels to go through.'

Jake realised he'd given the wrong idea. 'You've misunderstood,' he said. 'I didn't mean I wanted special treatment. I just wondered if you'd give me more details.'

Philips smiled wider, and took Jake's arm, turning him away from the gym.

'Actually, I think it's you who've misunderstood.' Phillips gave him a sly look. 'You see, marketing isn't about crossing the finish line first. Some people . . . well, they deserve special treatment. It all depends on what they're prepared to give in return. You follow me?'

Jake wasn't sure he did, but from the glint in Phillips's eyes and his lowered voice, Jake guessed he was being asked to give Phillips some sort of kickback.

'You're talking about something to sweeten the deal?' Jake whispered. 'Something in it for you?'

Phillips winked. 'Your words, not mine. I guess you know how it works, what with your dad being in the game too.'

Jake nodded. Hell, this guy was as slippery as an eel.

'I get it.' Jake reached for a bottle of the yellow Olympic Edge − Solar. 'Where can we talk about it further?'

Phillips climbed into the driver's seat of the cart. Jake caught the flash of a name on the bottom of his shoe, something Italian. 'Don't worry,' Phillips said. 'I'll come to you.'

'Hey, wait . . .' Jake started.

But Phillips was already driving away. Jake watched him go, frustration building.

So his suspicions were right. Phillips *was* as dodgy as he looked. But he was clever too. He hadn't promised anything, hadn't implicated himself. If he was effectively selling grants to the athletes − and that meant hundreds and thousands, if not millions of dollars − then that might explain why people were dying. Otto had been a handsome guy, full of potential. Definitely in line for the big time. Perhaps he'd refused to play ball with Edgar Phillips and paid the price.

Maybe Garcia had found out too. Jake felt the pieces fitting into place, even if the puzzle picture was still a bit fuzzy.

He walked back towards the dorm block, wondering if now was the time to tell his dad what he suspected. Or did his dad already have a theory of his own? Two deaths *and* him conveniently showing up were too much to be a coincidence.

First he needed to speak with Veronika.

As Jake passed the administration buildings, he saw two guys standing by the main doors keeping a lookout. Both were smoking cigarettes, despite the fact there were signs all over the complex saying it was strictly prohibited. Something about the way they stood, arrogant and threatening, primed Jake's senses: these guys looked suspicious.

The automatic doors of the admin building swished open, and a small figure in a pale suit walked out. The smokers crushed their cigarettes and hurried to catch up. One opened the door of a high-spec SUV. As the man climbed into the back seat, Jake froze.

It can't be!

He hadn't seen the face since St Petersburg.

It was Igor Popov.

9

Jake's feet were rooted to the ground. What the hell was Igor Popov doing at Olympic Advantage? He managed to move his legs, starting to run towards the administration building as the SUV rolled out of the parking lot. The windows were tinted black – he couldn't see inside. But he was sure. He'd recognise Popov's face anywhere after everything they'd been through. From the first moment he'd stepped into his dad's house in London, offering what seemed like a dream job coaching in St Petersburg, Jake had just known he was a criminal. And the way he'd dealt with his enemies since, brutally but never getting his hands dirty, had only confirmed that he was not to be messed with.

Jake burst through the doors into the admin building and straight up to the desk.

'Who was that man?' he asked.

The receptionist was busy buffing her nails and looked up

at him with a smile. 'What man, honey?'

'The one who just left,' Jake said.

The receptionist stopped inspecting her cuticles, and cocked her head at Jake. 'Say, you're the son of that soccer coach, aren't ya?'

Jake gritted his teeth. 'That's right. Steve Bastin's my dad.'

'He sure is cute,' the receptionist said. 'I don't mind saying I don't know much about soccer, but I might start watching it.'

Jake fought the urge to grab her manicure set and hurl it at the wall. 'Please,' he said, 'can you tell me who that was?'

'Well, I shouldn't really . . .' The receptionist pursed her lips. 'But perhaps you could do something for me first.'

'What?' Jake asked.

'The other girls would be really jealous if I managed to get a date with Steve Bastin,' she said, 'but I don't have his phone number . . .' She left it hanging.

Jake studied the woman. If his dad was keeping things from him again, Jake wasn't going to do *him* any favours. He leant over the counter and grabbed a pad and pen. He scribbled down his dad's mobile number.

'It's the least I can do,' Jake muttered. 'Just tell me, what was that man doing here?'

'You mean the German guy in the cream suit?'

'Russian,' Jake corrected. 'I think he's Russian. His name's Igor Popov, isn't it?'

'Yeah, that's right. *Parpov*,' she drawled. 'Why'd ya ask if you already seem to know?'

'But what is he doing here?' Jake asked, trying and failing to keep the growing annoyance out of his voice.

She folded the piece of paper with Jake's dad's phone number on it, and looked around conspiratorially. 'They treat him like a king around here. Must be one of the moneymen. He comes and goes as he pleases.'

'So he's been here before?' Jake asked.

'Oh, yes,' the receptionist said. 'Several times.'

Jake's watch bleeped. Ten minutes before he was due to meet Veronika at the track-and-field exhibition. He didn't think he was going to get much more out of the receptionist. 'Thanks,' he said. 'Do me a favour, though. Don't tell my dad where you got that number.'

Jake waited until half past two, but Veronika didn't show. Athletes and journalists were heading towards the stadium for the afternoon exhibition. Jake wondered if he'd got the wrong time, and tried to ring Veronika, only to get no answer. Jake hung up, silently cursing.

He saw her tennis friend, the Spanish girl called Maria,

walking past with a crowd of girls, all giggling.

'Hey, Maria,' Jake called. 'Have you seen Veronika?'

She shook her head, looking down her nose at Jake. 'Not since the morning practice,' she said. 'She left early. Said she had stuff to do.'

'Thanks,' Jake said.

She must be caught up with Krantz, he thought. But then Krantz walked past as well, speaking with a reporter who was holding up a Dictaphone.

Jake felt his nerves tense. Popov showed up, and Veronika disappeared, just like that. She'd said the guys in the 4x4 worked for some rich stalker. Did she have any idea how dangerous the Russian was?

As he entered the stadium, he told himself he was being paranoid. If he hadn't seen Igor Popov, then he wouldn't be worried. Veronika would show up soon.

But the lingering dread remained. Where Popov was involved, it paid to expect the worst.

Tan twisted his body in the air, releasing the pole, and cleared the bar by thirty centimetres. As he hit the mat, the crowd cheered, and no one harder than Jake.

'Go, Tan!' he shouted.

Jake had taken a seat away from the others to watch

his friend and the other track-and-field stars going through their paces. He'd half hoped that Veronika might be in here already, but he couldn't see her. Oz and his guys were sticking together on the opposite side of the stands.

Phillips had sat down with Krantz and a bunch of suits in the best seats. They were all drinking champagne, like it was a party or something. Jake was beginning to see that Olympic Advantage was as much about money and schmoozing as sport. And now that he'd learned Popov was involved, well, that only made it worse. Part of him wanted to call his dad and tell him he'd had enough, that he'd made a mistake ever coming to Florida. But a bigger part of him wanted to expose Olympic Advantage, and especially Phillips, for what they were.

Below, a coach with a megaphone announced to the crowd that the pole-vault bar was being set to six metres, just fourteen centimetres short of the world record. Jake couldn't believe it. Tan had told him most decathletes didn't reach their best until they were in their late twenties, and that vaulting was his least favourite event.

First came the women's 400m, though. The gun went off and four competitors burst out of the blocks.

Jake felt like that – running as fast as he could – but that he had no finish line in sight. *Where is Veronika? Was Krantz on the level? What if she'd overstepped the mark in questioning him; set off alarm bells? If I've got her mixed up in something . . .* But he couldn't finish the thought.

The girls were halfway round the track, and pushing each other close. A four-sided clock by the start line was ticking off the digital seconds. On the final bend, the girls were bunched, and two at the rear came together. One tripped and spilled sideways on to the grass, drawing an 'oooh' from the crowd. Jake was glad to see she got up unhurt. The rest of the pack streaked on towards the finish, with the front two girls shoulder to shoulder. As they reached the line, one lunged, taking first place by a matter of centimetres.

Amid cheers for the winner, Jake noticed one of the orderlies pointing at the stopped clock. It read 47.49 seconds. Practically a world record.

Perhaps there was something to be said for Olympic Edge, after all . . .

While the winner of the race did a victory lap, arms outstretched, Tan was rocking back and forth on the start line, in time with the crowd's clapping. Jake found himself leaning forwards in his seat.

Tan set off, his legs a blur as he reached sprinting speed, the pole lifted slightly from the horizontal. Whatever he was taking for his knee was clearly working. He hit the launch spot, and planted the pole. It took the strain, bending into a U-shape, then propelled Tan upwards. Again, he soared over the bar with perfect technique. The crowd went nuts, though Jake noticed that Phillips wasn't clapping, just grinning.

He's probably got dollar signs in front of his eyes, Jake thought.

The exhibition was to close with the high-jump event, and Jake could see Tan arguing with the orderlies below as they adjusted the pole-vaulting equipment. It was no surprise that he wanted another go.

Jake came down off the stands and walked up to his friend.

'Hey, Tan, that was awesome,' he said. 'You're on top form!'

'Yeah,' Tan said, pumped up and ready to go again, 'I ask for the bar higher, but they say no. I never feel better.' He turned back to the orderlies. 'Come on, guys, what you say? One more jump . . .'

'What about your knee?' Jake whispered. 'You were really pounding along the runway.'

Tan spun round, and pushed Jake in the shoulder, a bit too hard for it to be playful.

'Shut up,' he hissed.

'Hey, sorry,' Jake said, slightly taken aback. 'I'm just saying maybe you should take it easy. Save something for later.'

Tan's face slowly creased into a smile. 'No worries, Jake.

We celebrate, yes? You want to? How is football going? How things going with Veronika?'

Jake could hardly keep up with Tan's questions, but he guessed he was just high because things were going so well. 'It's all good.' He slapped Tan on the back. 'I'll catch you later, yeah?'

He left Tan arguing with the orderlies about his extra five centimetres.

Jake missed most of the rest of the exhibition because he was too busy keeping an eye out for Veronika. She never showed. He had to admit that he was officially worried. He left the stadium and decided to check out all the places he thought Veronika might be – her room, tennis courts, the canteen. He'd asked around. No one had seen or heard from her.

He was heading to the main entrance to ask the guards if they'd seen her when a red Lotus zoomed up behind him and stopped with a squeal of its brakes, only just missing him.

The window buzzed down, and he saw Phillips sitting in the driver's seat.

'Get in,' the marketing director said.

Jake hesitated. If Phillips was a killer, going for a ride with him might not be the smartest decision. But on the other hand Veronika was missing and he needed information.

'Get in before anyone sees you,' Phillips barked. 'We have to talk.'

Jake agreed. *What the hell* . . . He opened the door and climbed into the car.

10

As soon as the door closed, Jake started to feel edgy. Phillips pulled out of the complex and into the traffic, then drove south out of the town along the main street.

'Where are we going?' Jake asked.

Phillips didn't take his eyes off the road. 'Somewhere we can talk.'

When they took a turning, Jake recognised the road as the same one he'd driven along with Veronika the day before. As they passed the sign for Saddleback Swamp, Jake noticed that police tape still blocked the track.

'Sure was a pity about Pedro,' Phillips said.

Jake couldn't tell if he was being sarcastic or not.

'Yeah,' he replied.

They stopped at a truckers' diner about three miles from the complex. 'This'll do,' Phillips said.

Jake was glad to see a couple of the tables occupied by

truck drivers, one just with coffee, the other eating his way through a mountain of pancakes covered in maple syrup. Phillips wouldn't try anything here.

They walked along to a table at the far end, and sat facing one another in a booth. The waitress came to take their order. Phillips went for coffee; Jake ordered an orange juice.

'Have you thought about my offer?' Phillips asked.

Jake shrugged. 'I wasn't aware you'd made one.'

Phillips smiled as the waitress brought their drinks.

'I'll be straight with you, Jake,' he said, spooning three sugars into his cup and stirring slowly. 'You're a good-looking kid. Exactly the kind of face we want supporting the LGE brand.'

'Thanks,' Jake said, wondering where this was heading.

'I could get you a one-hundred-thousand-dollar grant by next week,' Phillips said. 'How does that sound to you?'

It *sounded* great, Jake thought, as he sipped his juice. 'What's the catch?'

Phillips took a slurp of his coffee, and dabbed his lips with a napkin. 'I'd want a fee, of course,' he said. 'Y'know, for oiling the wheels.'

'A fee?'

'Say ten gees.'

'Ten thousand dollars, yeah?'

'Yeah.'

So there it was. A simple backhander. Jake leant back in his chair and made a show of thinking about it.

'A hundred would be just the start,' Phillips continued. 'Perform well, and you'd be getting ten, twenty times that much on an annual basis. We're talking millions.'

'And you'd get a per cent?' Jake asked. 'For doing nothing?'

Phillips finished his coffee, his jaw tensing. 'Do I look like a crook to you?' Jake guessed the question was rhetorical. 'I'd come on board in an official capacity. Like an agent. You'd need someone to handle all that kind of stuff for you. Protect you from people who'd take advantage.'

Jake almost laughed out loud. Dodgy deals went on all the time in football. Backhanders, tapping up, agents playing one club off against another. He didn't doubt that Phillips could deliver on his promises, and the thought of all that money . . . He suddenly remembered what Otto had said to him just before he died − about not upsetting the moneymen.

'Did you make this same offer to Otto Kahn?' he asked.

Phillips took a deep breath through his nose, and steepled his fingers in front of his face. 'You ask a lot of questions.'

Jake didn't miss a beat. 'I'll take that as a yes. Let's just say I want to know who I'm doing business with.'

Phillips leant in closer. 'Too many questions can be dangerous.'

Jake held his stare until the waitress arrived at their table.

'Can I get you anything else?'

Phillips shook his head, still eyeballing Jake. 'Just the check, please.'

After he'd paid they walked outside into the heat. The wind had picked up, kicking little dust clouds around the parking lot.

'What do you say?' Phillips asked.

'Let me think about it,' Jake replied.

Phillips opened his door. 'Well, don't think too long. Some of the other kids have already agreed, and the door won't stay open forever. There are only a limited number of grants available.'

Jake climbed into the car. If it wasn't so far, he would have walked back to the camp. He'd spent about as much time with Phillips as he could handle.

As soon as they were in the car, Phillips tuned the radio to some awful country music station. Jake was glad he didn't have to make conversation. When they were a couple of hundred metres from the complex entrance, Phillips braked.

'You'd better get out here,' he said. 'We wouldn't want anyone getting the wrong idea, would we?'

Jake tried to smile. 'No, I guess not.'

As he closed the door behind him, Phillips leant over to the open window.

'Whatever you decide,' he said, 'this conversation never happened. Understood?'

Jake nodded. 'Understood.'

When Jake got back to the camp, he went straight to the dorm block. He was surprised to see Veronika standing outside the door to the building.

'Where the hell have you been?' she asked. 'I was worried to death.'

'Where've *I* been?' said Jake. 'We were supposed to meet at the exhibition, remember?'

Veronika frowned. 'I thought you said *after* the exhibition.'

Had he said that? He didn't think so, but he couldn't be sure. 'I hunted everywhere for you,' he said.

'Obviously not,' she said. 'I was in Maria's room.'

'She said she hadn't seen you since this morning.'

Veronika blushed. 'I meant Stacey, not Maria.'

'I rang your phone,' Jake said, not willing to let it go.

'Well, there must have been no signal.' She tossed her blonde hair and flashed Jake one of her killer smiles.

Jake was sure the hair-toss-smile combo was her way of

ending a discussion. She wasn't a good liar, but Jake guessed if she wanted to keep something private that was her business.

'Anyway,' she said, looping her arm through Jake's and leading him away from the dormitory, 'you'll never guess what I found out.'

'If it's half as good as what I got from Phillips, I'll be amazed,' he said.

'All right,' she said. 'You go first.'

As they wandered aimlessly around the complex, Jake told her everything, from following Phillips to the kiss with Dr Chow. By the time he got to Phillips's illicit offer in the diner, her mouth was gaping.

Veronika paused and turned to face Jake. 'You're sure he wasn't just offering to be your agent?'

'No way,' Jake said. 'He said he wanted a ten grand cut for putting me on the list. That's what we call a bung in my country.'

'I never did like that guy.' Veronika started walking again.

Jake jogged to catch up. 'Now your turn.'

'My meeting with Krantz wasn't quite so dodgy, but I did find out some interesting details.'

'Go on,' said Jake.

'Well, Krantz himself didn't have any time for me at all. I waited in his office for fifteen minutes, and then he came in and said he had back-to-back meetings for the rest of the day – but I managed to get some time with his secretary beforehand. She said Krantz has a lot riding on Olympic Advantage. Ninety per cent of the funding for the camp comes from sponsorship, right?'

'Like LGE,' Jake put in.

'And Ares Sports,' Veronika said. 'They're one of the biggest companies of sports merchandising in the world. Mostly in Asia at the moment, but spreading fast. Don't you think it's weird they don't have a bigger presence here?'

'I guess so,' Jake said. 'I thought they were like a silent partner.'

'Turns out that Ares have it written into the contract that Olympic Advantage must produce three medal-winning athletes within one year,' said Veronika.

'You mean athletes who are happy to promote Ares Sports,' said Jake, smiling. 'And if they don't?'

'Then Krantz is in a world of trouble.' Veronika cast a furtive glance around, then lowered her voice. 'While I was in his office, I checked a couple of drawers. It looks like Krantz has lots of debts. I think Olympic Advantage might be his last chance. If Ares pulls funding, he's got nothing.'

'Are you sure the secretary won't tell Krantz you were

sniffing around?' Jake asked, realising they were back at his dormitory, right where they had begun.

Veronika grinned. 'I promised to have a knockaround with her ten-year-old daughter. Anyway, it seems like Krantz is a desperate man.'

'It doesn't explain why he might want to kill anyone, though,' said Jake.

'Not yet,' Veronika admitted. 'But there's a lot of money up for grabs around here. It's like sharks to blood.'

Jake immediately thought of Igor Popov, and his reptile eyes.

'Vron,' he said. 'Your stalker – you need to be careful.'

She frowned. 'What do you mean?'

Jake took a deep breath. 'I've met him before – it's Igor Popov, isn't it?'

Veronika's eyes widened in surprise. 'How did you know?'

'It's a long story,' Jake said. 'But he's dangerous.'

'He's just a fan.' She took a few steps away from Jake. 'Harmless.'

'You should tell Krantz.'

'Please, Jake. Stay out of it.' Veronika's phone rang and she checked the screen with a frown. 'I gotta go. Catch you later.'

Jake watched her jog away, speaking into the phone.

While she was inside the complex, he doubted Popov could do much harm. So the Russian was a fan of tennis as well as football! But Jake knew he was a fan of money and power most of all.

Veronika turned and waved when she was a hundred metres away, still with the phone to her ear. Jake couldn't shake his suspicion that Veronika had something to hide.

He headed to his room, trying to fit the pieces together. Was it money that had got Otto and Coach Garcia killed, or had Phillips taken offence to Garcia hassling Dr Chow?

As he approached his door, he heard what sounded like someone shouting inside then a crash. He quickened his steps.

In the room, Tan was standing over his bed, angrily shoving clothes into his suitcase.

'What's going on?' Jake asked.

Tan jumped over the bed, eyes ablaze, and shoved Jake hard in the chest. 'You could not keep mouth shut! That's what!'

'Hey, calm down,' said Jake, raising his hands. 'I don't know what you're talking about.'

'Liar!' Tan shouted. 'I have visitor an hour before. Dr Chow.

She tell me she has no choice. End of programme for me.'

'Wh–why?'

'Why you think?' spat Tan, going to the drawer beside his bed and pulling out a packet of pills. He threw them at Jake, and they hit the wall beside his head. '*Someone* tell her about my knee.'

Jake had never seen Tan so angry. He'd seemed like the most easy-going guy at camp. Had that just been an act?

'I didn't say anything to anyone,' Jake protested.

Tan lunged at him again, this time getting his hand on Jake's throat and pushing him up against the door. 'You not tell truth!' he shouted.

Jake was a good six inches taller than Tan, and he guessed about twelve kilos heavier, but Tan was damn strong. Jake started to gasp. 'Get off me!' he croaked, but Tan only pressed harder.

Jake had no choice. He delivered a low rabbit-punch to Tan's gut. The decathlete doubled over with an *oomph*.

'What the hell?' Jake sputtered, creating distance between himself and Tan.

Tan stalked back to the bed. He drew the zip round his case, not looking at Jake. Then he yanked it off the bed and made for the door.

Jake stepped aside. 'Tan, wait . . .'

Tan turned on him, and shoved him viciously back into the wall.

'I not forget this, Jake Bastin,' he said.

Jake heard his footsteps disappear down the corridor, and the front door slam.

11

The next morning Jake was still shell-shocked by Tan's departure. He grabbed an energy bar and a few bananas from the canteen for breakfast, but decided not to hang around. Maybe he was being paranoid, but everyone – not just Oz and his goons – seemed to be staring at him and whispering.

I'm sick of all this, Jake thought. *All I want to do is play football. At least I'm good at that.* Jake was beginning to think that Olympic Advantage was all about money. And Tan's departure had only darkened the dark clouds hanging over the camp.

Jake decided to head over to the football pitch. Maybe a kick-about before practice would raise his spirits. As he passed the dorm block, he saw that his bedroom curtains were closed. *Weird*, he thought. *I'm sure I left them open.*

Had Tan come back? Jake checked his watch, and saw

he was going to be late, but something told him he'd better check it out. He jogged back to the dorm.

As Jake slipped in his key card and opened the door, he found the room cast in semi-darkness. Almost at the same time a sweet smell hit him. He flicked on the light.

'What the . . .?'

Tossed over his bed were a dozen bottles of Olympic Edge, all empty. The contents were soaking through the bedsheets and pooling in technicolour puddles on the floor. Someone had thrown all his clothes out of the wardrobe. They too were covered in the drink. Tan. Had he been angry enough to do something like this?

Jake walked further into the room, taking in the mess. He saw that someone had scrawled *No more questions* on the mirror in marker pen. Jake frowned. That didn't make sense – Tan didn't know anything about his investigations, did he?

Jake felt the hairs on the back of his neck prickle, and a split second later the wardrobe doors burst open. Out shot someone wearing a black hoodie and jeans, with a scarf pulled up over half his face. Jake tried to grab his arm, but the intruder shook free, and landed a glancing punch on Jake's jaw that snapped his head back and filled his vision with white. Jake fell backwards over a chair, and crumpled by the window.

He climbed to his feet as the guy bolted out of the door.

Jake lunged forwards but stumbled into the door frame; the punch had knocked him dizzy. He came out into the corridor and saw the attacker whip round the corner. Too tall to be Tan. A couple of other athletes were lounging at the end of the hall.

'Stop him!' Jake shouted, but they just looked up, barely moving at all. Jake set off in pursuit. By the time he got to the entrance to the dorm block, his attacker had thirty metres on him and was sprinting along the track towards the admin building and the complex's exit. Jake had shaken off the effects of the punch, and pounded after him.

You're not getting away from me, you bastard!

A clutch of cyclists was heading the other way, four abreast. The guy in the hoodie went straight through the middle, and they veered aside, crashing into one another and crying out calls of abuse. Three seconds later, Jake leapt over a fallen rider, shouting his apologies.

The front gates came into sight, and Jake grinned. The guards were standing there, checking a driver's ID. No chance anyone was getting out that way. The intruder must have seen it too, because he suddenly veered off, climbing a bank and ducking into some trees. Jake's legs were feeling it now. He leapt up on to the grass verge then into the woodland. Branches whipped his face as he tripped over roots and tree stumps.

'Stop!' he shouted, but the guy didn't let up. Did he even know where he was going?

They emerged on the other side by the rowing lake, and his attacker took the lakeside path towards the boathouses. Jake thought he'd made up ten metres. Two pairs of rowers were carrying their boats down to the water, hoisting them above their heads. The first couple planted their craft on the water, but those behind saw Jake coming and seemed to both pull separate ways. The attacker ducked beneath the boat, shoving one of the rowers out of the way. The rower fell backwards into the water with a scream, and the end of the boat smashed on to the stone jetty.

Jake steered a course round the outside, pursued by angry shouts. He saw a mesh fence ahead − the edge of the Olympic Advantage grounds. Beyond that was a patch of waste ground and then the car park for the town's supermarket. The hoodie threw himself at the fence and started to clamber up. Jake launched off the ground, and grabbed his leg. As the guy turned, Jake saw his eyes. Blue, and wide with fear. The intruder drew back his free leg and kicked out, catching Jake's knuckles. Jake fell back on to the ground with a thump, then watched his attacker scramble over the fence and into the car park beyond.

By the time Jake got to his feet, the hoodie was already

disappearing from sight among the cars. Jake had no chance of catching him now. He was panting for breath, and his jaw ached from the punch back in his room.

What the hell was all that *about?* he wondered. One thing was certain – if someone would go to this trouble to warn him off, then the events at the camp were no coincidence. And he wasn't giving up any time soon.

'You win some, you lose some,' he muttered to himself.

And now he was definitely late for practice.

Jake ran as quickly as he could to the football pitch. All the other players were passing balls between them, with Jake's dad at the centre overseeing things. When he saw Jake, he blew his whistle for everyone to stop. Oz's face broke into a malicious smirk.

'Where've you been, Jake?' he asked.

Jake wanted to get his dad on his own, to tell him what had happened. But he could just imagine what Oz and his pals would say to that. *Special treatment from the coach!* He'd have to take the flack.

'I'm sorry, Coach,' he said. 'I –'

'I don't want to hear excuses,' his dad interrupted. 'Everyone else made it on time.'

Oz had crossed his arms across his chest and nodded in smug satisfaction.

'Like I said, I'm sorry.'

'Not good enough,' his dad said, looking pained. 'I can't let this sort of attitude pass.'

Jake shrugged. 'Fine.'

So, Jake spent the entire football practice running laps, then stuck in goal. By the end, he was mad. His dad hadn't even given him a chance to explain himself. In fact, he came down harder than he would have on anyone else to prove a point. Afterwards, he made Jake collect all the other players' dirty kit and haul it in a sack to the laundry, even though they had the carts to do that. Well, Jake promised himself as he dumped the sack, when he finally cracked what was going on here, his dad would be sorry he hadn't listened.

By the time he came out of the showers with a towel wrapped round his waist, everyone else had cleared out. He went to his locker, and a voice spoke behind him.

'What I don't get, Baby, is why you even need the money.'

Jake turned to see Oz leaning against the tiled wall, staring into space.

'Get lost,' said Jake. This was the last thing he needed right now.

Oz glared at him. 'I mean, your dad's loaded. It must be nice to have your life handed to you on a silver platter. Bet he bought you that pretty watch, didn't he?'

Jake could feel his blood starting to boil. The mention of the watch – Popov's watch – only made him angrier still. He turned back to the locker, and pulled on his shirt.

'I know Phillips approached you too,' he said.

He felt a shove in his back, and fell forwards against the locker. *He's just trying to get a rise*, he told himself, turning to face his tormentor.

'I suggest you tell Phillips you're not interested,' said Oz, shoving him again.

Jake snapped. He grabbed Oz by the collar, and yanked him round so his back was against the lockers. He pulled back his fist and slammed it into the locker door just to the right of Oz's cheekbone. The sound echoed in the empty room.

'Careful who you threaten,' Jake said.

He heard noises out in the corridor, and Oz's eyes flicked that way. Jake let go as a group of baseball players entered, carrying mitts and bats. Oz straightened his collar and smiled confidently.

'Watch your back, daddy's boy,' said Oz, pushing past him and out of the door.

12

Over lunch Jake tried not to think too hard about his argument with Oz, and afterwards he had other things on his mind. Namely Veronika. In a swimsuit.

As part of the 'working together' ethos at the heart of Olympic Advantage, one day in each week was set aside for the athletes to cross-train in another discipline. It was a chance to try something new, and improve overall fitness. Jake had been about to choose baseball, but when he'd seen Veronika on the list for diving he'd changed his mind. He kidded himself that it was a chance to talk further about their investigations.

Now, balanced on the end of a diving board five metres up, he wished he'd chosen baseball after all. It looked a *long* way down. The water shimmered, and he could see the Olympic Edge logo detailed in tiles on the bottom of the pool.

'When you're ready, Jake,' said the diving coach, an attractive Canadian woman in a tight tracksuit.

I'll never be ready, thought Jake.

Veronika was standing at the end of the pool, wearing her swimming cap and doing stretches while talking to a Brazilian diver, a short, sinewy brunette called BeBe. Beside her, folding his arms with a grin like a Cheshire Cat, was his dad. When Jake had seen him outside the pool building before the session was due to start, his dad had apologised for treating him harshly earlier. Jake said he understood, even though it still rankled.

'Anyway, what are you doing here?' he'd asked.

'Oh, I wouldn't miss this for the world,' his dad said.

Five metres above the pool, Jake took a deep breath, bounced once, and leapt off the board. Gravity snatched him down, and he turned one somersault in the air before hitting the water in what could only be described as a mess. Water filled his nose and bubbles exploded around his head. Jake came up spluttering. Veronika and BeBe were both clapping and cheering.

'Go, Jake!' Veronika called.

His dad was shaking his head in bemusement. 'Very graceful,' he said. 'Almost swan-like.'

Jake felt himself go red with embarrassment, but laughed anyway. He front-crawled to the end of the pool, and pulled himself out.

'Not bad,' BeBe said, 'but you must keep your arms close to your side. That way you will not splash so much.'

'Yeah, right,' Jake said, still shaking the water from his ears.

'Seriously, I think you got water on the ceiling,' his dad added.

'Ha, ha,' Jake said. 'Your turn, Vron.'

Veronika walked to the other end of the pool, while a male diver took the steps up to the ten-metre board. With perfect poise, he executed a double twist and hit the water like a knife cutting through butter.

'I've got a little way to go yet,' Jake muttered.

His dad had wandered off and was talking with the diving coach.

Veronika walked along the board in small, tentative steps. Even in an all-in-one, she looked good: lithe and poised, with toned shoulders and legs that seemed to go on forever. Just the sort of athlete LGE would pay a fortune for.

'Just take it easy,' the coach called. 'Nothing too elaborate.'

Veronika nodded, lifted her arms above her head, and jumped. She rolled backwards, hands straight by her sides, and opened out into a pretty straight dive. She came up beaming.

'You're a natural,' BeBe called.

Veronika stepped out of the pool, and took off her

swimming cap, letting her hair drape over her shoulders.

'We've got a pool at home,' she said apologetically.

BeBe leant down, unzipped her bag and took out a water bottle filled with what looked like apple juice. She took a swig, then offered it to Veronika.

'Try it. It is a special mix I put together. Ginseng, lemon and some few herbs.'

Veronika took a sip, and nodded. 'It's really good. Better than Olympic Edge.'

'I hate that stuff,' BeBe said. 'If it is natural, then my grandmother was a mermaid.' She held the bottle out to Jake. Before he could take it, another hand reached in and snatched it away. Dr Chow had appeared from nowhere, and glowered at them all.

'I'll take that,' she said. 'You all know the rules about unauthorised supplements at the camp.' She opened the bottle and sniffed the contents. 'A word please, BeBe.'

The diver rolled her eyes and followed Dr Chow towards the door to the changing rooms.

'Dr Frankenstein strikes again,' Veronika said. 'Hey, you're up, Jake.'

Jake climbed up to the board, determined to do better this time. From on high he could see the whole pool area. Veronika was cleaning her goggles. By the changing room,

Dr Chow was pointing to the bottle in her hand, and by her wild gestures Jake guessed the word she was having with BeBe wasn't a quiet one. She opened a door to an office and beckoned BeBe inside. Jake's gaze passed over the spectator stand, then fixed on one face in particular.

Igor Popov was sitting in the back row.

Jake's dad hadn't noticed the Russian. He leant in closer to the diving coach, who was playing with her hair. Jake forgot about his poise, and jumped off the board, hitting the water feet first. He swam as quickly as possible to the far end, scrambled out and ran to his dad.

The coach saw him coming. 'Hey, no running in here!'

Jake ignored her. 'Dad,' he hissed, gripping his father's arm. 'Look!'

'What is it?' he asked, annoyed.

Jake pointed up at the stands. Popov was gone.

'What's the matter with you, Jake?' his dad asked. He glanced at the diving coach apologetically.

'Popov was there,' said Jake under his breath.

'Popov?' his dad said, frowning, and cast a furtive glance from side to side. 'Don't be silly, Jake. Igor Popov's in Russia.'

'I swear,' Jake said. 'I saw him the other day too.'

'If this is some sort of joke, it's not funny.'

'But —'

'Enough,' his dad said. He lowered his voice. 'Not here. We can talk about this later.' He turned back to the diving coach.

As Jake rejoined Veronika, his eyes kept searching the stands. Popov was definitely gone. *If he was ever there*, thought Jake. Perhaps the punch to the chin had messed with his head.

BeBe called over to them from the top of the ten-metre board. 'Hey, guys, I will show you how to do it?'

'Is it just me,' Jake said, 'or is BeBe a little bit annoying? I'd like to see her take a corner.'

'Or serve and volley,' Veronika laughed.

BeBe bounced on the balls of her feet once, twice, three times, then sprung upwards, a good four feet.

She's too close to the board, Jake thought. She turned a half-pike in the air, but as she came down her head hit the diving board with a crack that sounded across the hall and made Jake's stomach turn. BeBe lost all shape in the air and slammed into the water side-on, her limbs sprawling. Someone screamed.

Jake was in the pool without thinking, swimming as fast as he could towards where the Brazilian was floating face-down. He swam through red-tinged water, and turned BeBe upright, doing his best to support her neck. Her eyes were closed, and blood poured over her face from a cut under her hairline.

'Don't touch her!' the coach shouted. 'Let the paramedics handle this.'

Jake waited, carefully cradling BeBe until the paramedics took over. They pulled BeBe from the water, and Jake pulled himself out, feeling numb.

Veronika rushed to his side. 'Not again,' she muttered.

The paramedics started mouth to mouth, and more people gathered in a hushed circle. BeBe was limp, her skin already bleached white. As her blood drained off over the slick poolside tiles, Jake knew she was dead.

13

Veronika's eyes filled with tears as Jake put his arm round her. Dr Chow knelt beside the body with the paramedics, feeling for a pulse. The towel under BeBe's head was soaked pink with blood and water. They'd tried to resuscitate her for close to a quarter of an hour, but now Dr Chow shook her head.

'I'm sorry, Mandy,' she said to the diving coach. 'She's gone.'

The diving coach wailed, and placed a hand over her mouth.

'I need everyone to leave,' Dr Chow said. 'Now.'

Jake and Veronika filed away to the changing rooms. At the door, she mumbled, 'This can't be happening.'

'It is happening,' Jake said, coming to his senses. 'And I know who's to blame. Igor Popov.'

'Not that again,' Veronika said. 'You talk about that guy like he's Satan.'

'As close as,' said Jake. 'If sport has an underbelly, he's

there – trust me. I saw him at the pool today. He's a gangster, a murderer . . .'

'Hey, chill out,' she said. 'He's just a sports fan. I think you're getting a bit James Bond on me and, honestly, it's a bit immature. Let's deal with the facts and not some crazy conspiracy theory.'

She walked off into the female changing room, leaving Jake feeling like an idiot. *Immature?* Where had that come from? She didn't know Popov like he did. She hadn't seen what that bastard did to people who got in his way. Olympic Advantage was becoming more dangerous by the hour.

Following the events at the pool, Krantz had convened an emergency meeting in the gym hall and had broken the news that everyone had already heard: another athlete was dead. He had looked harassed as he told of the latest 'tragedy' to befall the camp.

His face was lined with worry, and he announced that forthwith the guards at the front gate had been instructed not to let anyone enter or leave the camp except for police. It was complete lockdown until investigations had run their course, and they'd be called up one by one to make statements.

'I'm sure it's just procedure,' Krantz added. 'And, needless to say, I want you all to cooperate entirely.'

Jake raised his hand. 'Do the police have any formal suspects?' he asked.

Krantz's face darkened and he gave an uneasy smile. 'I think I've made it perfectly clear, Mr Bastin, that the events at Olympic Advantage are tragic accidents, and nothing more.' He addressed the crowd again. 'And now we'll have a minute's silence in memory of those we've lost.'

As Jake bowed his head along with the other athletes, he almost found himself feeling sorry for Krantz. If what Veronika had found out was true, this could be the end of the road for the camp director. No wonder he was doing everything he could to focus attention away from the murderer in their midst.

Jake could've lived without seeing Detective Merski's face again. The guy looked as if he hadn't slept or changed his clothes since the last time they met at the swamp.

'Well, what a surprise,' he said. 'Take a seat, Jack.'

'It's Jake.'

'Park it,' said Merski.

Jake took a seat in the makeshift interview room in the complex's admin buildings.

'So, Jake,' said Merski. 'How's it feel to be the chief suspect in a homicide investigation?'

'What?' Jake said.

Merski clasped his meaty fists on the table, and Jake got a whiff of body odour.

'Look at it from my point of view,' the detective said. 'We have three people dead, and you're the nearest thing to a connection I got. You were at two of the deaths, and you miraculously stumbled across the third. Looks suspicious, doesn't it?'

Jake could tell Merski was trying to get a rise out of him. What was this guy's problem?

'Only if you're the suspicious type,' Jake muttered, though as he said it he realised something else: Veronika had been at all the crime scenes too. In fact, she'd been up to Saddleback Swamp before they'd visited together. He pushed the thought away. *Now who's getting suspicious?*

'Don't get smart with me, kid,' Merski snapped. 'I got enough to take you in.'

'Then why don't you?' Jake asked. 'I'll tell you why. Because you know it's ridiculous. It's taken you guys five days to work out there might be something going on here.'

Merski's face broke into an ugly grin. 'I suppose you have a theory?'

Jake wanted nothing more than to mention Popov's name, but he couldn't. His dad, and MI6, would go mad if he brought heat on to the Russian. The best thing to do would be to keep the detectives off his case so he could keep investigating the deaths himself, with or without his dad's help.

'No,' he said. 'I haven't.'

'I heard you were friends with this BeBe kid?' said Merski, leaning back in his chair.

'Not really,' said Jake. 'I've spoken to her a couple of times.'

'That's not what I heard,' the detective said. He looked at a pad of paper covered in illegible handwriting. 'Says here that you might have had a little crush on our victim.'

Jake didn't know if he was lying or not. 'You're kidding, right?'

Merski raised his eyebrows. 'Do I look like the kidding type? One of your footballing buddies told me.'

Oz! It had to be. He couldn't believe that Oz was willing to dump him in the middle of a murder investigation. This was way beyond sporting rivalry.

'Well, they told you wrong,' Jake said.

Merski sighed. 'We're going to need to talk with you again,' Merski said. 'So don't go getting itchy feet.'

Jake nodded, but he knew he wasn't just going to wait around until someone else died or the murders got pinned on him.

Next morning as he left the dorm, Jake saw that security had been stepped up. Two-person patrols were making their way around the camp, and he was even asked to show his ID to a guard he'd seen a dozen times already.

'I've been here since day one,' he said.

'I'm afraid it's the new regulations,' the guard said. 'We had a couple of reporters trying to sneak in last night over the back fence.'

Jake pocketed his camp ID, and headed to the canteen. The noticeboard outside said the track practice and a couple of the scheduled circuit sessions had been cancelled at short notice. It seemed some of the trainers had decided it wasn't worth the risk. Whether they meant to themselves, or to the athletes, Jake didn't know.

The mood over breakfast was subdued. Some of the South American athletes, friends of BeBe, were already talking about packing up and going home. But most people in the canteen thought the police investigation was a waste of time over 'a massive coincidence', or so Jake heard more than once.

Veronika came in late, looking tired, and Jake scooted along his bench to give her somewhere to sit. She walked straight past him with her tray carrying a half-finished bottle of Olympic Edge, and went to sit instead with Maria. *Suit yourself*, he thought.

But as he was leaving, he decided to stop by her table.

'Hey, Vron,' he said. 'Do you fancy going for a jog later?'

'We're playing later,' Maria interjected.

'I wasn't asking you,' Jake said. 'Veronika?'

She faced him wearily. 'Like she said, we've got a match later.' Veronika stood up, grabbing her bottle of Olympic Edge. 'Just leave me alone, Jake.' She walked out of the canteen leaving the rest of her breakfast untouched.

Jake heard a snigger behind him, and saw Oz leaning against the wall, rolling a toothpick between his teeth.

Leave it, Jake said to himself, following her out. He could do without Oz this morning.

Near the stadium, he came face to face with his dad.

'Hey, Jake, some of the other players are already inside. I want to have a practice, see if we can't breathe some life back into the camp.'

'Great choice of words, Dad,' Jake muttered.

His dad gave them all a talk before they split into teams, casting doubt on the end-of-camp game versus the US team. Apparently with the shadows hanging over Olympic Advantage, the sponsor wasn't sure it was the right thing to do. That brought groans from the players, but Jake found he hardly cared. This was turning out to be the summer camp from hell.

Oz's team members were their usual bullish selves, pulling

Jake's shirt, or tripping him off the ball when his dad was looking the other way. Even when Oz raked his studs down the side of Jake's leg, he managed not to react, and just picked himself up.

After forty minutes, Jake's team was 2–0 down. Rafe slid a perfect through ball between two defenders and Jake was all clear on goal, one on one with the keeper. He stepped over twice, then tried to feint left. Somehow the ball got stuck under his feet, and rolled to the keeper.

'Wake up, Jake!' his dad shouted. 'That should have been two–one.'

Jake held up a hand to apologise to his team-mates, and jogged back upfield.

His team was down to 4–1 by the time ninety minutes was approaching, and Jake missed a header from close-range, bringing another round of cursing from the other players.

'A headless chicken could have put that in,' Rafe said.

When the final whistle went, Jake traipsed off with the rest of the team.

A hand caught his shoulder.

'Hold it right there, mister,' said his dad.

Jake shrugged the hand off. A couple of the other players had turned to stare.

'What's wrong with you?' said his dad under his breath. 'You're playing like this doesn't matter.'

'Does it?' said Jake. 'Dad, three people have died, in case you haven't noticed. Popov's hanging around, but you seem more interested in pulling me up for off-side.'

'Not Popov again,' his dad said, rolling his eyes.

Jake started to walk away, but his dad jogged up alongside him. They reached the edge of the gym block. Jake glared at the couple of players who'd stuck around to watch and they disappeared inside.

'OK,' said his dad. 'It's true that Popov's an investor in the camp, but this time you're barking up the wrong tree, Jake. Popov just happens to own a controlling stake in a major sponsor called Ares Sports.'

Jake took a moment to process what his dad was telling him. If Popov ran Ares, then he had a hold over Krantz. The pieces of this jigsaw puzzle had just been thrown in the air.

'And I suppose you being here is just a coincidence,' Jake said. 'You must think I'm really thick, Dad.'

His dad took a deep breath and cast a quick glance left and right. 'OK, I'll be straight with you. My superiors have got me here in an observation role, but nothing more. With so many up-and-coming athletes in the same place, there's a lot of international scrutiny.'

'So I'm just your cover,' Jake blurted. 'I knew it.'

His dad sighed. 'No, you're my son and, for the last time, I had nothing to do with you being invited. My bosses told me to come out here, and they aren't the kind of people you say no to. But that was after you were approached in Milan.'

Jake thought about what Veronika had said about Krantz, and how much pressure he was under from Ares Sports. He thought about Phillips and his dodgy offers, the kiss with Dr Chow, and Garcia showing up dead after an argument. If anyone had been keeping things to himself, it was Jake. Perhaps it was time to get the pros on board.

'You're wrong,' he told his dad. 'There is something going on.'

'Go on,' his dad said. 'Tell me your theory.'

He told his dad everything, from his first day at the camp to seeing Popov at the pool the day before. In going over all the details again, he realised he still didn't really know what was going on, other than money was involved, and lots of it. His dad kept a calm face, but when Jake got to the part about getting into Phillips's car and driving out of town he shook his head.

'Christ, imagine what you could have been walking into,' he said. 'You should have come to me.'

'I didn't want to worry you unless it was something important,' Jake said.

'This is my fault. Your mum was right. I shouldn't have let you come. If I'd known about Popov –'

'Well, I'm here now,' Jake said. 'What do we do next?'

'We do nothing,' his dad said. 'I'm sorry, Jake, but I can't let you stay at the camp.'

'What?' Jake couldn't believe what he was hearing. After everything they'd been through together in the last few months. 'You've got to be kidding me. I *trusted* you!'

'This isn't about trust,' his dad said. 'It's about keeping you safe.'

Jake spun round, and saw a bottle of Olympic Edge upright on the turf. What a joke! He wished he'd never laid eyes on the disgusting stuff. It was a symbol of everything that was wrong with this money–driven world of sports, the pointless merchandising, the corruption . . .

Swinging his boot, Jake blasted the bottle against a wall. It exploded in a blue shower.

'There's no need to lose your temper,' his dad said.

But Jake was staring at the dripping wall, and the bottle emptying out the last of its contents on the grass. Maybe it was his dad mentioning his temper, but the image of Tan getting in his face in the dorm sprang to mind. The guy had erupted like a volcano. This was the friend who up till then had done everything he could to avoid getting into fights.

'Jake . . .' his dad was saying.

'Wait a minute,' Jake said, picking up the busted bottle. Tan had guzzled the stuff, hadn't he? And Veronika had snapped at him that very morning, right after drinking it. Most of the people at the camp seemed to like it − and with Phillips pressing it into every empty hand, it was hard to avoid. And, come to think of it, the other footballers had become more aggressive too.

Jake's mind raced through the possibilities. Could there be something in the drink that messed with the chemical balance in your body? Something that drove normal people to violence? Garcia's car had been full of empty bottles, but the police had focused on the alcohol. What if they'd got it wrong? What if it was the Olympic Edge that had literally driven him over the edge and made him crash into the swamp?

'It all adds up,' he muttered, half to himself.

'What does?' asked his dad.

'And Otto too,' Jake continued. 'He drank bottles of this stuff right before he dropped the barbell.'

'What are you talking about, Jake?'

'Dad, I think there's something wrong with the drink.' He went through his suspicions. The only one that didn't add up was BeBe, but perhaps that was a genuine accident.

He expected his dad to dismiss it out of hand, but instead he said, 'It might be worth investigating.'

'We've got to tell Dr Chow,' Jake said. 'Get her to tell people to stop drinking the stuff.'

'Not yet,' his dad said. 'We don't want to go ringing alarm bells.'

'Well, we'd better find out pretty quick,' said Jake.

His dad nodded. 'I know just the place. Let me make a call.'

14

J ake and his dad waited at the back of the service buildings
as the laundry truck pulled in. With police still interviewing
everyone and security patrols tighter than normal, there was
only one way out.

'If we get caught now, it's going to look really bad,' his
dad said.

'You're not prime suspect number one,' Jake said. 'Can't
you call someone at MI6 and sort something out?'

'That's not how it works, Jake,' his dad said. 'I'm not sure
the Americans even know MI6 has someone here. We can't
jeopardise my cover for a hunch.'

Jake gave him a hard glare.

'OK, an educated hunch, but still a hunch.' Jake's dad
looked around again. 'You ready?'

Jake nodded.

A Hispanic guy in a brown uniform jumped out of the truck

and went to open the back doors. He waved to two maids, who were already wheeling out tall cage trolleys full of dirty laundry.

'What's going on?' the truck driver asked the maids. 'They asked to see my ID at the gate. I said, "Carl, it's me, Roberto!" but he said there's been another accident. The police are here . . .'

One maid explained the situation as Roberto lowered the platform at the back of the van and loaded in the trolleys. Another maid gave her version of events, and the trio headed into the service building still chattering away.

'Come on,' said Jake, leading the way. He and his dad hopped up into the back of the van and crept to the far end. They positioned themselves behind the trolleys, and pressed up against the front of the van. It was a tight squeeze. Jake had a rucksack containing three bottles of Olympic Advantage.

Roberto loaded on several more trolleys, and seconds later the engine rumbled to life. Jake gripped the edge of a trolley to stop himself being thrown around the van as it lurched round corners. As they pulled to a halt, Jake guessed they'd reached the front gates of the complex.

A voice rose above the hum of the truck: 'Boss says we need to check the back.'

Jake's gut tightened as he held his breath.

'You're kidding me,' said the driver.

''Fraid not, Robbie.'

'Well, if you want to check my dirty laundry, you're welcome,' said Roberto, laughing. Jake expected light to flood in at any moment.

'He's right,' said another voice. 'This is BS. Let him through.'

'Thanks, guys,' said Roberto. 'See you in a couple of days. Hopefully Alcatraz will have chilled out by then.'

The guards' laughs were drowned as the engine revved and they were on their way again. Jake breathed out. Too close.

They drove for about five minutes. The smell of stale sweat and body odour was overwhelming. Jake tried to hold his breath. When Roberto killed the engine, they heard his door open, and footsteps round the side of the van.

'Now!' His dad pointed to the hatch leading through from the rear into the driver's area. Jake went first, squeezing through into the passenger seat and gasping for fresh air. The back doors of the truck opened as his dad slid through after him. Roberto had left the driver's door open, and Jake peered out into a yard. They were at the rear of a building, and steam was spiralling out of several vents. Empty laundry carts were stacked near a wide set of double doors.

Jake couldn't see anyone around. Beyond was a side

street lined with cars. He signalled for his dad to follow, and they climbed out of the truck and darted across the yard. In less than thirty seconds they were on the street, just a father and son out for a stroll.

'Where are we going exactly?' Jake asked.

'Curiosity killed the cat,' his dad said as he hailed a cab. They climbed in. 'Hannigan's, corner of Southwest Seventh Avenue and Fourth,' he said.

'You sure?' said the driver, eying them in the mirror. 'Wouldn't think it's your kind of place. You look, well, too sober.'

'I'm sure,' his dad insisted.

They drove across the city and into an area of rundown condos and cracked pavements with weeds sprouting up between. Even the sun looked a little less bright on this side of town. Many of the shops were closed with faded graffiti sprayed on metal shutters. The streets were mostly empty except for clusters of dodgy men hanging around the street corners.

The cab driver pulled up outside a shuttered bar with a giant green shamrock hanging over the door. 'I'd like to say "enjoy yourself",' said the driver, 'but I think that'd be a long shot.'

Once Jake's dad had paid and they'd both climbed out, the cab beat a speedy retreat. 'What is this place?' Jake asked.

'It's a state-of-the-art covert surveillance facility, jointly

127

operated by the CIA and MI6,' his dad deadpanned as he walked inside.

It took Jake's eyes a moment to adjust to the gloom of the interior. There were a couple of customers hunched over their drinks at separate tables. They'd probably been there long enough to gather dust.

The girl behind the bar was Japanese, but she must have been wearing contacts because her eyes were an unsettling blue shimmer in the bar lowlights.

'Hey, Steve,' she said. The accent was pure London.

'Francesca,' his dad said, kissing her on both cheeks. 'Beautiful, as always.'

'Why, thank you,' she said, beaming. 'Doesn't hurt to make an effort, even if the surroundings leave something to be desired.' She waved a perfectly manicured hand round the bar. 'Rick's waiting for you.'

Jake stared at the rest of the clientele. That would have to be some serious undercover if any of these guys were spooks.

Jake's dad led the way past the end of the bar and through a curtain. There was an old-fashioned service lift at the end of a corridor littered with crates of empty beer bottles. A mop and bucket were propped up in one corner, and the whole place smelled of stale booze and cigarette smoke.

Jake's dad pulled aside the bars on the lift, and climbed

inside. It creaked ominously. 'You coming?' he asked.

Jake took a tentative step to stand beside his father. 'You sure this is safe?'

'Nope.' His dad slammed the bars shut with a little too much gusto.

There was a switch-box dangling from a cable, and his dad thumbed a large red button. The lift juddered into life and Jake's stomach lurched.

'State of the art,' he joked.

They must have gone down at least two floors. Jake watched exposed pipe-work and wiring pass, and the air chilled. This was no ordinary pub.

With a clank, the lift stopped. His dad pulled aside the doors, and Jake stared into darkness. Then with a series of low *woomph*s bright white strobes flicked on along the ceiling, illuminating a spotless corridor. At the end stood a man wearing a lab coat. He looked like something from a seventies science programme. A shaggy brown beard, long lank hair and moustache. His glasses must have been two centimetres thick, and his eyes swam behind them like fish in a tank.

'Steve Bastin,' he grumbled in an American accent. 'What took you so damn long?'

15

'**G**ood to see you too, Rick', Jake's dad said. 'This is my son, Jake. Don't worry, he has clearance'.

'Looks like you, poor kid.' The scientist gave Jake's dad a friendly clap on the back. 'Come into my office.'

They followed Rick through into his 'office', which resembled something out of *CSI: Miami*. Everything was pristine stainless steel. Three huge computer screens hung side by side, one switched off, the other reeling data in some kind of code and the other displaying a complex line graph. Jake recognised all the normal equipment from the science labs at school – a centrifuge, microscopes, test tubes and pipettes. Jars of chemicals were arranged on shelves.

'To what misfortune do I owe this visit?' Rick asked. Up close, Jake saw dark smudges under his eyes. The guy was like a zombie. Jake assumed it was from the lack of natural light, and sleep probably.

'We need a chemical profile on this liquid,' Jake's dad said. Jake fished out three bottles of different Olympic Edge flavours and held them out to the scientist.

Rick inspected the bottles over the top of his glasses. 'Kids'll drink anything these days, won't they? I'll get you the results by tomorrow.'

'We need it now,' Jake said, without thinking. 'People are dying . . .'

'People die all the time.' Rick glowered at Jake.

'Please,' Jake's dad said. 'I'll owe you, Rick.'

The scientist smiled for the first time since Jake had met him. 'Well, if you put it that way. I've been trying to fix up a date with Fran. She seems to like you. Maybe you could help . . .'

Jake tried to keep a straight face, but had to pretend he was searching for something else in his bag.

'I'll put in a good word,' his dad said.

Over the next hour Rick went from one side of the lab to the other, fetching test tubes, dripping Olympic Edge from the three bottles on to slides and examining them through microscopes then running samples through something he called a mass spectrometer. A lot of the time he seemed to move in slow motion, as if he was walking through water. Jake was getting frustrated and shot the occasional glance at his father that said: *What's taking him so long!*

The effect wasn't helped by Rick's constant drawling. He was the kind of man who spoke as if he didn't care if you were listening or not. Having whinged for a good fifteen minutes about Francesca, he was now talking about a conspiracy-theory convention he'd recently visited in Atlanta. Apparently some loons thought that Lady Gaga's latest album had brainwave-altering, mind-control properties.

Jake tried to tune him out, but his dad nodded or made a sound every so often. Clearly patience was a key skill for a spy.

Finally, a machine in the corner let out a series of beeps, followed by three sheets of paper. 'Let's see what we got,' Rick said.

He laid the papers out side by side on a bench, and Jake and his dad leant over.

The sheets were filled with numbers and code, measure-ments in units Jake didn't recognise.

'Do you mind?' the scientist said. 'You're in my light.' Jake and his dad backed off a little. 'Very curious,' continued Rick. He removed his glasses. 'Very curious indeed. You say this stuff's supposed to be organic?'

'That's what they told us,' Jake answered.

'Well, they told you wrong,' Rick said. 'The flavourings are natural, but the strange thing is that all three bottles have different levels of several ingredients that I can't identify. If they were from the same batch, you'd expect the ingredient levels to be the same. There are a lot of additives. Some steroid compounds, definitely.'

'Steroids?' Jake asked. 'So they'd improve performance?'

'Hard to tell,' Rick said. 'But nothing illegal.'

'Harmful, though?' Jake's dad asked.

'Again, nothing conclusive,' Rick said. 'I'd have to get complete data, and that means getting HQ involved. It's certainly not deadly in these sorts of doses. I can get some more details to you later, but it'll take at least forty-eight hours.'

Jake's heart sank. 'But people are dying. It must be poisonous.'

Rick stared at him. 'Look, kid, I don't teach you how to play soccer, do I? Leave the science to me.'

Jake's dad got a cab to drop them back on Main Street near to the complex.

'So what do we do for forty-eight hours?' Jake asked. 'People are still drinking that stuff and we don't really know what's in it.'

'We do nothing,' his dad said. 'You heard what Rick said – there's nothing illegal in it.'

'But Rick only tested three of the flavours. Maybe it's one of the others that causes people to get ill.'

'I think you're grasping at straws,' said his dad. 'First we need to get back into the stadium without being spotted.'

'Too late,' Jake said. Veronika was crossing the street towards them, with a frown on her face.

When she was close enough, she asked, 'How'd you get out?'

'I could ask you the same question,' Jake said.

'They lifted the lockdown,' Veronika said. 'The detectives said they'll continue their enquiries, but they couldn't keep us locked up forever. The camp can carry on.'

'Hey, I'll give you guys some privacy,' said Jake's dad, backing away.

'Wait, Dad,' said Jake. 'We haven't finished discussing –'

'I'll catch you later,' his father said. 'Don't worry. I'll take it from here.'

'Dad!' But he was already walking away. *Thanks a lot*, Jake thought.

'You've been investigating without me, haven't you?' said Veronika, her eyes narrowing.

Jake decided to tell her the truth. So what if Rick hadn't

found anything deadly. Olympic Edge wasn't what it seemed. It wasn't all natural, and it was laced with steroids and who knows what else.

'I think the deaths might have something to do with Olympic Edge,' he said.

'We know that already,' Veronika said. 'People stand to make a lot of money.'

'No, I mean the drink itself,' Jake explained. 'I don't think you should drink any more of it. Remember how Otto was knocking it back right before he was killed? And the bottles in Garcia's car?'

'Sure,' said Veronika, 'but I've been drinking it for days, and I'm fine. Playing better than ever, actually.'

'What if it makes some people better, but is harmful to others? Or maybe only some of the flavours are bad. Or there might be a tipping point. Y'know, too much and it's bye-bye.'

Veronika shrugged. 'Could be, I suppose, but that seems pretty unlikely.'

'We need to get some answers,' Jake said, 'and I think I know just the place.' He pulled out Edgar Phillips's card. It listed the address of LGE's Florida office, at a business park just outside the city. 'You up for it?'

'I don't think they'll let us just walk in and rifle through the files,' said Veronika.

'Good job we've had plenty of practice sneaking around, then,' said Jake.

'We can take my car.' Veronika gestured to the ice-blue Porsche parked a half block away.

The Liquid Gold Energy offices were hard to miss. A skyscraper glittering in the afternoon sunlight, with the letters LGE four storeys tall near the roof. It towered above the surrounding buildings. Stepping out of the air-conditioned Porsche, Jake felt the heat baking off the tarmac of the car park. He could hear sirens in the distance.

'If there is something dodgy about the drink, they're not going to want to admit it,' Veronika said.

'Agreed,' said Jake. 'We need to be clever.'

They crossed the car park and a set of corporate gardens. A sprinkler was firing spray over the glistening grass. Jake was dazzled by how pristine the place was – this was the clean side of money, away from the dirty underbelly. As they walked, two people in business suits hurried past them at almost a run. Jake noticed people at a lot of the windows too, all staring at something just ahead.

'What's going on?' Jake broke into a jog.

They rounded the wall at the end of the gardens, and saw an ambulance parked up alongside two police cars near the entrance to the LGE block. A crowd of at least fifty people had gathered, and were being pushed back as the police drew a cordon tape across the front. Some people looked upwards, pointing and muttering.

Jake pushed through the crowd, and came face to face with a uniformed cop. He got a firm shove in the chest.

'Get back!' said the cop. 'Let us do our job.'

Jake peered behind the police officer. A sheet had been pulled over a motionless body on the ground. It wasn't big enough to cover the blood spatter as well.

Not another one! thought Jake.

'Who is it?' Veronika asked.

'It's Ed,' said a woman with a handkerchief clutched over her face.

'He was the marketing director,' said a suited man. 'Jumped off the roof.'

Ed? 'Edgar Phillips?' Jake said.

16

A gust of wind blew across the entrance to the LGE offices, catching the edge of the sheet covering the body. The sole of one of the dead man's shoes appeared, and Jake made out the word *Mancino* embossed in the leather. No doubt. It was Phillips.

'I can't believe it,' said Veronika, shaking her head. 'I saw him leave the complex earlier. He seemed fine.'

Dr Chow stepped out from behind the ambulance, talking with a paramedic. Her eyes were red and when she saw the body she burst into fresh tears and buried her face in the paramedic's chest. Jake remembered the kiss he'd seen behind the medical centre and felt a rush of sympathy. He hadn't liked Phillips, but he and Dr Chow had obviously been close.

When Dr Chow saw Jake, she seemed startled, and took a deep breath to regain her composure, then walked over.

'Jake, Veronika,' she said, suddenly businesslike, 'you shouldn't be here. You –' Her face crumpled, and she covered her mouth.

'I'm really sorry for your loss, Dr Chow,' Jake said, not knowing where to look.

'Oh, it's terrible,' she sobbed. 'I was supposed to meet Ed . . . Mr Phillips, for lunch. I was late. If only I'd arrived . . . if only.' She buried her face in both hands as the tears flowed.

'Come on,' Jake said to Veronika. 'We should leave.'

He turned to go, but Veronika didn't. 'Why would he kill himself?' she asked, a little too briskly for Jake's liking.

'Vron,' he whispered. 'Now's not the time . . .'

'Dr Chow,' Veronika pressed, reaching for the doctor's elbow.

Dr Chow glanced up once more. She sniffed deeply.

'The police are saying he had a note pinned to his chest,' she said, 'but I can't believe it.'

'A suicide note?' Veronika asked.

Jeez, Jake thought, *the woman's just lost her boyfriend. Go easy on her*.

Jake thought he saw a flash of fire in Dr Chow's eyes that quickly died. She nodded. 'Apparently he claimed responsibility for all the deaths at the camp – something to do with financial irregularities. He thought the police were on to him. But I can't . . . I *won't* believe it.' She took a few sniffs. 'Anyway, you shouldn't really be here.' She squinted at Jake and Veronika as if she was seeing them for the first time. 'What *are* you doing here?'

Jake spotted a brown sedan cruising slowly towards the building. *Damn!* Merski.

'We should be getting back.' Jake grabbed Veronika by the arm and pulled her through the crowd, keeping bodies between them and the detective's car.

'Hey! What are you doing?' Veronika said, pulling free.

Jake pointed through the crowd, as Merski was heaving his bulk out of the driver's door. The sweat patches under his arms stretched almost down to his waist.

'We *really* don't want to be found at another crime scene,' he said.

'This isn't a crime scene,' said Veronika. 'Phillips committed suicide.'

'Maybe the police won't see it like that,' said Jake.

As Jake and Veronika took the long way back to her car, past more office workers hurrying to get a glimpse of a dead body, he wondered if he even believed the suicide story. Phillips was rotten to the core, so was he really the sort of guy who'd feel so guilty about 'financial irregularities'?

*

Dinner at the camp was delayed as all the athletes were again summoned to the gym hall for an impromptu announcement. Merski and his colleague stood behind the podium as Krantz told everyone the case was officially closed.

'The sad death of our colleague Edgar Phillips has brought the answers we were all searching for. I'm pleased to say the camp can now continue as normal, and we can all get back to what we do best: honest, competitive sport.'

Jake saw Krantz fighting to keep the smile spreading across his face.

'The worst thing we could do,' continued Krantz, 'is let the tragic deaths of Otto Kahn, BeBe Erquidez and Pedro Garcia cloud our own efforts to excel. For their sake as much as our own, let's carry on.'

A round of applause echoed through the hall, but Jake didn't feel like clapping. Of course Krantz was happy. With Phillips conveniently claiming responsibility, the heat was off the real culprit. And he, the director, could fulfil his obligations and dig himself out of a financial black hole.

Phillips's suicide didn't add up. It seemed too convenient. And no one seemed to know exactly why Phillips had killed each of his supposed victims.

Out of the corner of his eye, Jake saw Veronika leaving

through a side door of the hall with her mobile phone to her ear. Merski had taken the podium and was telling the other athletes that there'd be lots of media interest in what had happened at the camp, but that they should be wary of talking to journalists.

Jake left the hall after Veronika. Outside, he couldn't locate her at first. Jake was about to turn back when he spotted her. She was standing beside the same 4x4 that had been hanging around since the start of the camp. Jake could see the window was wound down and Veronika was gesturing wildly and shouting at the person inside, but Jake couldn't hear her words. A hand shot out and tried to grab her, but she backed off and started to walk away. Next, two guys emerged from the back doors of the vehicle and hurried after her.

That's enough! thought Jake. He ran down the verge into the car park as the first of the guys tried to steer Veronika back to the 4x4.

'Hey! Get off her!' Jake shouted as he approached.

She saw him. 'No, Jake,' she said. 'Not now.'

The two thugs each grabbed one of Veronika's arms. They looked at Jake then back to the car, as if waiting for instructions. They were both built like juggernauts, but Jake hardly felt any fear. Veronika tried to twist free of the thug's iron grip. Jake wasted no time. Once he reached Veronika, he swung his foot into the first guy's groin and the man folded like a house of cards on to his knees with a moan. Veronika stumbled back, free from her attackers. Jake faced the second, fists raised.

'Jake, you don't understand,' said Veronika, stepping between him and the remaining guy.

Jake ignored her. 'Let the girl alone,' he told the one guy still standing.

'It's OK, Jake.' She took a step closer to him. 'Please just stay out of this.' Jake could see that she was scared.

'You should listen to the girl,' said a Russian voice behind him.

Jake spun round as the car door opened. Igor Popov climbed out.

He wore the same pale suit as the last time Jake had caught sight of him. His skin was almost white, as if he'd been keeping out of the sun. Jake hadn't seen the Russian up close since the day in St Petersburg when he'd casually mentioned the deaths of Christian Truman and his son. Jake knew Popov was responsible for the Trumans' deaths, even though no one could ever prove it.

'I knew you were caught up in all this,' Jake said.

'This is none of your business,' said Popov. 'I want you to leave us alone, Mr Bastin.'

'Wait!' said Veronika. 'You two know each other?'

Popov's eyes glittered. 'You might say that.'

'Just get the hell out of here before I call security,' said Jake. 'Leave Veronika alone. What are you? Some pathetic old stalker?'

The thug who Jake had kicked eyeballed him with malicious intent.

Popov smiled, and his gaze shifted to Veronika. 'Stalker? I've been called worse. Do you want to tell him, sweetheart, or shall I?'

Jake found the way he said 'sweetheart' sickening. 'Tell me what?'

Veronika sighed. 'I didn't want you to get involved in all this.' She lowered her gaze, her cheeks flushing red. 'Jake, meet my dad.'

17

Jake felt as if he'd been punched in the gut. Then slapped about the face for good measure. He glanced from Veronika to Popov, then back again. He searched both faces for a resemblance, but it just wasn't there. Veronika sounded as Californian as they came.

'No way,' he mumbled.

Popov nodded, and the thug next to Veronika retreated back to his side like a good guard dog.

'It's true,' Veronika said, giving Popov a hard stare. 'I lied about only seeing my dad a couple of times a year. Until five days ago, we'd never even met. I've lived with my mom in LA my whole life. She wanted nothing to do with *him*.'

'Tell me about it,' Jake said.

'When I heard my daughter was going to be attending the camp, I thought it would be a good opportunity to make contact,' Popov explained, shuffling his foot slightly.

Jake had never seen him so meek.

'And I've told my *dad* that he can shove his newfound interest up his ass,' Veronika said through gritted teeth.

'You only need time,' Popov said. 'I'm your father. I care about you. I can open all sorts of doors for you, my dear . . .'

'I've done OK on my own, thanks,' she snarled back.

Popov opened the door to the 4x4 and beckoned inside. 'Perhaps we should go for a drive.'

'Screw you.' Veronika stomped away across the car park towards her car. Jake stared at Popov for a few more seconds, then went after her.

'Veronika, wait!' he called. She didn't break her stride as she climbed into her car, and started the engine. Jake reached for the handle on the passenger side, but heard the click of the central locking.

With a screech of rubber, the Porsche sped off. Popov waved to Jake and climbed casually into the 4x4. Soon Jake was all alone in the car park. *Goodbye and good riddance to all the Popovs*, Jake thought. *How could I have been so wrong about her?*

Back in his room, Jake kicked a ball at the wall over and over. So much for Veronika Richardson. She had Popov's blood running through her veins. He'd trusted her absolutely, told her everything, but she'd been keeping the biggest secret of all. What else had she been hiding from him? Maybe she was more mixed up in this than he thought.

He started doing kick-ups, trying to get his thoughts in order. Did his dad know who Veronika really was? Could MI6 really *not* know that Igor Popov had a daughter living in the States? Especially as she was on the verge of making it big . . . He'd thought he was getting closer to answers about what was happening at Olympic Advantage, but he couldn't trust anyone.

The door to his room opened. Veronika came in, holding a bottle of white Olympic Edge.

'You could have knocked,' Jake said. 'I thought I told you not to drink that stuff.'

'I'll do what I like,' she said, taking a gulp. 'And you're hardly one to talk about intruding on other people's privacy. What did you think you were doing?'

Jake retrieved the ball from her feet. 'I want you to leave,' he said. 'Now.'

'We need to talk,' she said.

Jake turned towards the window. 'Why? So you can lie to me some more?'

'I haven't lied to you,' Veronika said.

'You forgot to mention your dad is a Russian gangster.'

'Hey! Don't talk about him like that! You know nothing about him.'

'Ha!' Jake laughed bitterly. 'I know I can't trust him. Just like I can't trust you.'

'Is that right?' she said. 'Just because I didn't feel ready to share my family troubles? Don't be such an immature little *boy*!'

Jake rounded on her. 'You don't know Popov like I do,' he said. 'He's scum!'

His words seemed to hit her like a blow, and she rocked back on her heels. 'He might not be perfect,' she said quietly, 'but he's not the monster you make him out to be.'

'I don't care!' spat Jake. 'Your dad's a killer. A low-life crook. Don't you see –'

Veronika's hand caught his cheek in a vicious slap that sounded like a whip-crack. Half a second later the burn spread across the side of his face. There were tears in Veronika's eyes.

'You're a liar. You're no better than your father,' Jake said.

Veronika started to tremble, and saliva was gathering in the corners of her mouth. The bottle of Olympic Edge fell out of her hand, and her eyes rolled back in her head.

'Vron?'

Jake saw her knees buckle, and he leapt to catch her.

He eased her down on to the floor. Her whole body started to shake violently, and her fingernails dug into his arm like talons. Jake tried to hold her steady with one arm, and with the other reached into her mouth to stop her swallowing her own tongue.

'Vron,' he repeated. 'Can you hear me?'

A strange rattling noise was coming from her throat, but gradually the convulsions died. Jake rolled her into the recovery position, then checked the pulse in her throat. Her heart was thumping at close to one-eighty, but her breathing was shallow. It had to be the drink.

Jake scooped her into his arms and went to the door. As soon as he was in the corridor, he shouted at the top of his voice. 'Someone call an ambulance.' Heads poked out of various doors along the corridor. 'Don't just stand there!' he yelled. 'Call 911!'

'She's in a stable condition, but still unconscious,' the emergency doctor said, closing the door to Room E12 behind him. Jake peered through the viewing panel and saw Veronika lying on a bed with her eyes closed. She had tubes in both arms and a mask over her face.

I can't lose her now, Jake thought, but no one was listening to him, not the paramedics on the ambulance ride over, not the emergency room staff. 'I'm telling you,' said Jake. 'It's whatever's in the drink. Olympic Edge.'

'And I've already told you,' said the doctor, 'a sports drink couldn't have this effect, even if you drank a whole lake's worth.'

'At least run some tests,' Jake said. 'There are hundreds of bottles of this stuff at the camp.'

'Enough!' said the doctor, signalling to a passing security guard. 'We'll run the standard toxicology tests to see what this girl has put into herself, but I won't be lectured by a kid with an overactive imagination.' He turned to the security guard. 'Take this young man out of here. He's not family and he's getting in the way. If he makes any trouble, call the police.'

Jake was gripped by a vice-like hand. 'What's it gonna be, kid? Easy or hard?'

Jake let himself be led away, and waves of hopelessness crashed over him with each step away from Veronika. Why wouldn't the doctor listen?

He was pushed out into the ambulance bay at the front of the hospital. It was getting dark, and the complex was a good forty-minute walk back through the city to the camp. Jake wished he'd remembered to bring his mobile phone. It had been such a rush to get Veronika to hospital, he hadn't even picked up his wallet, so there was no way he could make a call to his dad. Jake set off at a run, letting his frustration drive his legs. He would have loved to see Krantz's face right then. So much for the case being wrapped up. The guy didn't deserve to stay afloat after just brushing everything under the carpet like that.

Jake took a route down a deserted road lined with a lock-up facility of low-rise storage units. He presumed it must lead back to Main Street. He needed to speak with his dad again, get Rick to carry out more tests. He *must* have missed something.

Jake suddenly heard footsteps right behind him. He half-turned as something hit him hard near the base of his spine. A stinging surge spread across his body.

Everything went white.

Jake woke up with the smell of leather in his nostrils. His vision swam into focus, and he realised he was in the back of a car, lying awkwardly across a seat. He managed to sit up, but his whole skeleton seemed to ache. Sitting opposite him was Igor Popov and the guy Jake had dropped with a kick to the balls.

'You bastard!'

Weakly he tried to lunge, but the thug leant forwards and pushed him back into his seat. He waved something that looked like a police truncheon. As he pressed a button, the end fizzled with silver electricity.

'I didn't ask Kurt to use his little toy,' said Popov, folding his hands between his knees, 'but I think he rather enjoys it. I think you should relax, Mr Bastin.'

Jake's head was pounding. 'Your daughter's in hospital,' he said. 'What do you want with me?'

Popov flinched. 'Well, Jake, I find myself in an unusual position. You see, I need your help.'

'You'll be waiting a long time.' Jake sat up straight.

'I thought you might say that,' said the Russian, 'which is why I had to resort to such —' he waved his hand towards the stun-rod — 'clumsy measures. Jake, I fear that someone is using the Olympic Advantage athletes as guinea pigs, testing illegal performance-enhancing drugs concealed within the supposedly organic energy drink.'

Jake's eyes widened. 'I know,' he said. 'Trouble is no one else believes it.'

'I don't yet know who is behind all this,' said Popov, 'or even *why* they are doing it, but the last thing I want is for any more athletes to get sick. Or worse.'

Jake considered the Russian for a long moment, but he wasn't buying Popov's pure motives. 'Because Ares Sports might suffer too.'

Popov glared at him. 'So that my daughter doesn't die,' he said. 'We need to find out what they're putting in the drink, and then we need to find an antidote.'

Jake held Popov's stare. *We?* Could he really trust this man, after everything that had happened in Russia and Italy? True, Veronika had changed the stakes considerably, but he wouldn't put it past Popov to treat a daughter he'd hardly met as collateral damage in a bigger plot.

'This *Phillips*,' Popov said the name as if it tasted rotten, 'cannot have been working alone.'

'I don't think Phillips was involved at all,' said Jake. 'He was corrupt, but not a murderer.'

'So, do we have a deal?'

Jake stretched his back – the lower half felt badly bruised.

'I need an answer, Mr Bastin . . .' said Popov.

Did he really have a choice? Maybe Popov's people could find something that Rick had missed.

'Only if, when this is all over, we let the authorities deal with whoever is responsible. I've seen your brand of justice before.'

Popov grinned like a wolf, and held out a hand. 'Understood,' he said. 'I just want to see my daughter well again.'

Jake stared at the hand. What would his dad think about this?

Popov must have been reading his mind. 'Oh, and I don't

think there's any need to worry Bastin Senior with any of this, is there?'

Jake took Popov's hand in his. 'Of course not,' said Jake, lying through his teeth.

It was dark by the time Popov pulled up in front of the gates of the complex. The thug handed Jake a mobile phone. 'That's to call me,' said Popov, 'in case you find anything important.'

Jake pocketed the phone, and started to get out of the car, but something stopped him. 'How did you know where to find me?'

Popov glanced at the watch on Jake's wrist. 'I like to keep my friends close but my enemies closer.' Popov grinned his devilish grin again. 'My little gift to you was not without its benefits. It's got a tracking device so I'll always know where to find you.'

Jake went to remove his watch. He didn't like the idea of the Russian keeping tabs on him.

'Keep it for a little while longer. Now that we are working together, it might come in handy. You never know when you might need me.'

Jake reluctantly nodded and walked back into the camp without looking back. He'd agreed to share information with a master criminal. Just who was Jake Bastin working for now? He thought of Veronika in her hospital bed, barely alive.

You're working for her.

Back in his room, Jake washed his hands several times, but still thought he could feel Popov's touch, smooth as snakeskin. He'd sworn to himself in Milan that he'd never trust him again.

But sometimes you had to deal with the devil to get things done.

18

After breakfast, Krantz called all the athletes together in the main stadium over the tannoy. There was to be a combined training session in aid of bringing the camp closer together. It was like he'd forgotten a certain tennis star was lying in hospital less than three miles across town.

As Jake ran out in his training kit at ten o'clock, he saw his dad talking to a small group of athletes in the stadium grounds. In total there were close to two hundred at Olympic Advantage and they were now all scattered around. At least he wouldn't have to be up close to Oz this morning.

At least half the athletes were holding or swigging bottles of Olympic Edge. Jake didn't get it: a lot of these young men and women had been drinking it for over a week. There was no pattern. Otto had been huge, BeBe small. Completely different lifestyles and sports. The Brazilian said she didn't even drink the stuff. But there was definitely something wrong with Olympic Edge; even Rick didn't seem to understand what was in it.

'All right, everybody, get together,' called his dad. 'My name is Steve.' He caught Jake's eye and gave him a friendly nod – at least he hadn't mentioned his surname. 'We're going to mix things up a bit today: fast and slow, strength and agility, stamina and power. I expect we'll see some interesting contrasts between your respective disciplines. We'll get things started the old-fashioned way, though, with a few light laps. I need a pacemaker.' He pointed to Oz. 'Ellman, you'll do. Keep it gentle, yes?'

As they set off round the track at a light jog, Jake wondered what the point was. A lot of the others were chatting to each other, but he kept quiet. He really wanted to speak with Dr Chow – she'd been tasked with measuring the effects of Olympic Edge, and she'd lost someone close to her. Maybe the doctors at the hospital would listen to her?

Jake felt a shove in his back, but ignored it. They were running bunched up, so it was inevitable.

'Get out of the way!'

Jake twisted, expecting to see one of Oz's pals, but it was a gymnast, a Canadian guy called Adam Lee whom Jake had spoken to a couple of times with Tan. His eyes were wild, and despite the slow pace he was dripping with sweat.

'We're supposed to be taking it slow,' said another runner.

Lee launched forwards, practically clambering over the people in front. People started to grumble:

'Watch where you're going!'

'Slow down, man!'

But Lee wasn't listening. He broke through the front of the pack, shouldering Oz aside, and sending him sprawling. Normally Jake wouldn't have minded seeing the Australian take a spill, but something was wrong. Lee continued to charge ahead.

'Stop him!' Jake yelled.

Dom broke away after Lee. If anyone could catch him, it would be the Jamaican sprinter. But just as he was getting close, the Canadian jerked sideways, veering off the track and across the central field. It looked like he was sprinting for a gold medal. The rest of the pack had come to a halt.

Jake saw his dad from the other side of the track, running as fast as his false limp would allow to intercept Lee. With his head down, arms and legs pumping, the gymnast didn't see Steve Bastin until Jake's dad rugby tackled him in the middle, bringing him to the ground in a blur of tangled limbs.

Jake ran across. At first, he thought they were fighting on the ground as Lee thrashed and his dad tried to hold the gymnast down, but as Jake drew closer he could see Lee's eyes were shut and he was frothing at the mouth.

'Give me a hand!' shouted his dad.

Jake knelt on the grass and managed to control the gymnast's bucking legs. One of Lee's arms came free and he slammed his fist into the ground so hard Jake thought he'd break every bone in his hand. Jake managed to grab the flailing arm, but he tore it loose again, and Jake was left holding a beaded bracelet on a leather thong from his wrist.

'What's going on?' asked Oz, his voice full of uncertainty.

'Phone an ambulance,' said Jake. 'And get Dr Chow!'

Lee was gurgling, and blood was coming out of his nose. Jake wasn't sure if it was internal bleeding, or if he'd managed to hit himself. With a final, shuddering convulsion, Lee flopped, suddenly still. His head flopped back, and his eyes were closed.

'Let's take him inside,' said his dad, lifting him by the shoulders. Jake took Lee's feet, and together they hoisted him up. They hurried across the field as quickly as they could, with a loose group following them.

Jake could already feel Lee's skin going cold beneath his touch.

Ten minutes later, with only Jake and his dad looking on, Dr Chow was breathing heavily from her attempts at resuscitation. She hunched over Lee's body, which they'd laid across a table-tennis table, pumping his chest. 'Come on!' she said. 'Breathe!'

Jake's dad had made the others wait outside, for fear of crowding the doctor, but Jake thought she was fighting a losing battle.

'Let me try,' said his dad.

Dr Chow looked over. 'I'm a doctor,' she said accusingly.

'Don't worry,' said his dad. 'I'm trained. And, to put it bluntly, you need to be strong to carry out a prolonged resuscitation like this.'

Jake caught a flash of annoyance in Dr Chow's face, but she stepped aside as his dad took up the position, and began the rhythmic compressions. After a minute he stopped and placed two fingers to Lee's throat. 'I've got a pulse!'

Jake realised he'd been holding his breath and let it out.

'Thank God!' said Dr Chow.

Jake's dad held his hand over Lee's slightly open mouth. 'He's breathing too,' he said. He rolled Lee into the recovery position as the sound of sirens came from outside.

'I'll show them the way,' he said to Dr Chow, leading Jake outside.

She stood over Lee, one hand protectively on his shoulder. 'Thank you,' she said. 'Thank you so much.'

A crowd of the other runners had gathered outside the

sports studio, and his dad ran over to the ambulance and the paramedics who were gathering their things. Then Jake realised he was still gripping Lee's snapped bracelet. Some of the crowd were shaking their heads in disbelief; others were crying quietly. Jake went back inside the studio to drop it off. He knew it was sentimental, but it seemed like the right thing to do.

At the door to the table-tennis courts, Jake paused for a moment to peer through the wire-mesh viewing panel.

The doctor was leaning over Lee's body, still gripping his upper arm. In her other hand was a syringe.

'Out of the way, please,' said a voice behind him. 'Coming through.'

Jake moved as the paramedics entered the studio hall.

'Everything OK?' asked his dad, drawing up behind him.

'I'm not sure . . .' said Jake.

'He's going into shock!' said the paramedic.

Jake turned back to the room. Lee was spasming on the table, his legs thrashing, and his back arching. One of the paramedics tried to support his head while the other lay over his body. Dr Chow had stepped away, her hand over her mouth.

Jake tried to push into the room, but his dad pulled him back. 'Let them work, son.'

161

'But, Dad –'

'No buts. He's in the best hands now.'

Jake didn't bother to protest. He'd heard the same steel in his dad's voice before and he knew there was no point arguing.

A short while later, the paramedics wheeled out a covered gurney. Jake placed the beads on one side beside Lee's body. He remembered watching the gymnast on his first day in the camp. He'd been completing a routine on the parallel bars with amazing fluidity and strength. He'd seemed like a nice guy too. All that potential, just snuffed out. He doubted whether the camp could possibly continue now, even if Krantz wanted it to.

Most of the other athletes were peeling off in small groups. *They must be getting used to death by now*, Jake thought.

His dad's face was grim. 'We need to talk,' he said to Jake. 'In private.'

Together they walked quickly back towards the admin buildings, and his dad led him up into the office which had been Coach Garcia's.

'Just wait here,' he said.

'What are you going to do?' Jake asked.

'Get in touch with my superiors,' his dad said. 'They've

picked up increased phone activity from Igor Popov. We need more manpower. More surveillance.'

'Dad, I don't think Popov's involved this time. I think Dr Chow might be up to something. '

'Stay out of it, Jake.'

'But I saw her injecting something before the paramedics arrived. In Lee's arm!'

'Enough, Jake. It was probably adrenalin. Standard procedure. I'm taking you away from here. It's not safe.' He was pacing the room. 'I'm going to make sure personally that Krantz stops people drinking any more of that stuff. Stay here while I make some calls.'

As soon as his dad had left the room, Jake wandered over to the window. He knew he'd seen something strange.

A cold sensation crept over Jake's skin.

Why did Dr Chow even have a syringe on her in the first place? She must have known she'd need it. Jake gazed across from his dad's office on the first floor towards the table-tennis studio. The ambulance was pulling away.

A second later, Dr Chow herself came out and stood for a moment, watching it drive off. Her hand went into her pocket, feeling something there. *The syringe*. She walked briskly to one of the golf buggies. She climbed in and drove off.

How had he missed it before? Of course it was her! She'd

been pushing the Olympic Edge almost as much as Phillips. She'd argued with Garcia in the bar the day before he died in the swamp. Jake's mind was working fast, flicking from image to image. And who'd been the last person to see BeBe before she climbed the board for her final dive? It was Dr Chow, Jake recalled. She'd taken the girl from Brazil into one of the changing rooms. She'd been angry about BeBe's energy drink. Just what had happened behind that door?

Jake could have thumped himself as he bolted down the stairs and dashed past the receptionist. She shouted something about his father but he didn't bother to stop. He'd let everything distract him up till now: Oz Ellman, his dad, Phillips, the argument with Tan.

Dr Chow had even been at the scene when Phillips had taken the quickest way down from the twenty-third floor of the LGE building. The truth had been right before Jake's eyes all along.

19

J ake ran across the grass. The medical centre was on the other side of the complex, and it would take a good ten minutes to get there. He tried to control the thumping in his chest. By the velodrome, something beeped in his kitbag. It took a second to realise it was the phone Popov had given him. Jake fished it out and hit the answer button.

'Hello?'

'Mr Popov hears another athlete has died,' said a Russian voice.

'How's Veronika?' Jake asked.

'Mr Popov wants you to know his daughter's condition is deteriorating. What have you found out?'

'I think that Dr Chow is responsible,' said Jake. 'I don't know why yet.'

Some muffled conversation echoed down the line, then Popov's voice came on.

'Jake, what is happening?' he asked in a panicked voice.

'Someone else has died,' said Jake.

'I don't care about that,' he said. 'You need to find the antidote. Veronika's getting worse.'

'I'm doing everything I can!' Jake insisted.

'Well, do it quickly,' Popov said. 'If she dies, I'll hold you personally responsible.'

The line went dead.

Jake saw a couple of bikes leaning up against the gate to the cycling track. Their riders were doing stretches a few metres away. Jake ran up, and seized one of the bikes by the handlebars.

'Hey, you can't do that!' shouted a cyclist.

'Sorry, man, it's an emergency,' said Jake, throwing his leg over the seat, and pushing off.

The bike's owner tried to grab him, but Jake darted out of the way.

'Come back!' called the other.

Jake juddered down a set of concrete steps, and narrowly missed a reversing golf buggy. Jumping up on to a kerb, he steered between the dorm blocks and across the grass.

He skidded up outside the medical centre and ditched the bike. Dr Chow's golf cart was already parked up. Jake pushed the door open on to a quiet corridor with treatment rooms off either side. He went straight to the room at the end: Dr Chow's laboratory. Without knocking, he burst through the double swing doors.

The doctor was by the sink, emptying sample tubes full of colourless liquid down the drain. She frowned when she saw him, but carried on with what she was doing.

'Can I help you?' she asked.

'Perhaps I can help you?' said Jake. 'Destroy some more of the evidence, maybe?'

The doors stopped swinging behind him.

'I don't know what you're talking about,' she said, crossing the lab with the empty tubes in a rack. 'I'm just making some space in here. The police are sure to want me to act as consultant for Adam's post-mortem.'

Jake wasn't fooled. She was *too* cool.

'I guess you'd like that, wouldn't you?' he said. 'To cover your tracks. What did you put into Adam? Some sort of masking agent?'

'You've got a vivid imagination,' she replied.

Jake kept his back to the door. Somehow this woman – all five foot three of her – had killed Garcia and Phillips. They'd underestimated her, and Jake wasn't about to make the same mistake. He could smell the sickly tang of Olympic Edge in the air.

'There's no doubt it works,' said Jake, trying to stay calm. 'Whatever you've been putting into that drink does something special.'

Dr Chow leant back against the counter and smiled in a way Jake hadn't seen before. Arrogant. 'Thanks,' she said.

'Shame it kills people too,' said Jake.

Her smile vanished. 'You can't prove that,' she said. 'The police could test almost every bottle in this place, and they'd find nothing. That's the beauty of my experiments.'

'Almost every bottle?' Jake said.

Dr Chow's eyes shifted for a second to the fridge across the room. A single, unmarked bottle, filled with clear liquid, stood on top.

'And you killed Coach Garcia and Phillips because they found out?' said Jake.

'Pedro thought he could blackmail me,' she said. 'He wanted a slice of the pie. All it took was a little injection and the alligators did the rest.'

'And Phillips?' said Jake. 'I saw you kissing. I guess you were just using him to get access to Olympic Edge.'

'Poor Eddie.' Dr Chow's mock concern was nauseating. 'Not as stupid as he seemed, and too damn nosy for his own good. I quite liked him. For a while.'

'So much that you pushed him off the roof,' Jake spat.

168

Dr Chow laughed. 'After I slipped some of my special mixture in his coffee, he didn't take much persuasion. He wanted some fresh air, and that's exactly what I gave him.'

Jake moved a few steps sideways towards the fridge. If he was right, that bottle contained all the evidence he needed.

'No one's going to want an energy drink that kills them,' he said.

'I've made a few mistakes, sure,' said Dr Chow, 'but it's just a question of balance. It seems to have given people a bit of a temper, even in small doses.'

'It drives them crazy,' said Jake, remembering all the fights and the violence on the pitch.

'A minor side-effect,' said Dr Chow. 'Imagine a world where one drink can make an amateur athlete twice as good, and a good athlete Olympic standard.'

'It sounds like cheating to me,' said Jake. 'A shortcut without the hard work.'

Chow laughed. 'You're so naive it hurts. What do you think sport is, apart from hunting for an advantage? You don't see tennis players with wooden rackets, do you? Or runners with old-fashioned pumps? Athletics is all about finding the edge, and soon I'll have the right formula for a safe and legal route to victory. They'll give me the Nobel Prize for chemistry.'

'I'm not sure they award the Nobel Prize to people in jail,' said Jake. He picked the bottle up off the counter. When he turned again, Dr Chow was pointing a gun at his chest.

'You're not going anywhere with that,' she said. 'That's my extra-strength mixture for people who ask too many questions.'

'I guess this is what you gave to BeBe and Veronika,' he replied, staring at the gun.

'BeBe threatened to call the authorities and Veronika was asking too many questions.'

He tightened his grip on the bottle, the evidence. He knew it held Veronika's only chance of survival. 'And what about Otto and Adam?'

'They were just greedy,' said Dr Chow. 'Guzzled too much before I'd worked out how to perfect it.'

'So they die because of your mistakes?'

'All scientific breakthroughs come at a cost,' said Chow. 'Looks like you'll be donating your body to medical science. It's for the greater good.' She took aim at Jake's head.

'If you fire that in here, someone will hear,' Jake blurted, and took a step away from her.

'I'll say you attacked me. I'm not sure Detective Merski needs more evidence that you're bad news.'

Jake glanced at the door. If Dr Chow was a good shot,

she'd take him down easily. And the cops would probably believe her story.

Jake saw her arm tense a split second before she pulled the trigger. He jerked aside as the bullet ricocheted off the wall. He darted to the door. The doctor swung the gun around again. The crack of a bullet split the air as he dived through the double doors and into the corridor. Running towards the exit, he felt something wet on his arm, and wondered if he'd been shot. He heard Dr Chow's footsteps behind, and the notice board to his left exploded in a shower of glass.

'Come back here!' she screamed. Jake pushed through the main door into the sunshine and realised he felt no pain. It wasn't blood on his arm; it was liquid from the bottle, leaking fast from two holes in the base where the bullet must have passed. Jake watched helplessly as the vital evidence spilled away.

Without thinking, he lifted it to his lips and swallowed great mouthfuls of the clear fluid. It didn't taste like the Olympic Edge he'd drunk on the first day. This stuff was thicker, like watered-down syrup, and the taste was metallic. Almost at once, he felt a warmth spreading across his chest, and his blood seemed to pump harder through his veins, buzzing right to the tips of his fingers and toes. What the hell was this stuff?

Dr Chow came through the main doors, and pointed the

gun at Jake. He dodged behind the golf cart as the bullet crack sounded, and it whacked off the pavement.

He dived behind the building, running towards a low wall at the back. It was about one and a half metres high, but he vaulted it, barely using his hands for support. His whole body felt lighter, and more agile.

The adrenalin flooded Jake's system like a tidal wave of raw power. All he knew was that he had to get to Hannigan's. Rick was the only person who could help him, or Veronika, now.

Jake ran for his life.

20

Jake's heart was thumping like a steam engine in his chest, so hard it felt it might burst through his ribs at any moment. But his skin was cold. He gritted his teeth and fought the urge to scream. What on earth had he done to himself?

An alarm started going off across the complex, a wailing clarion. Dr Chow must have hit some sort of security button. She'd be telling security to stop Jake Bastin at this very moment. He wouldn't let that happen. He knew that if he slowed down the poisons inside him would take over, and he'd meet the same fate as Adam Lee, convulsing until he died.

Jake saw a detachment of three security guys on his right. One pointed and they began to run to intercept him. There was no way he'd be able to get through the front gates if they were locked. Suddenly he remembered chasing his attacker the other day beside the boating lake. As he reached a practice sandpit, a meaty security guard dived at Jake's legs.

He put on a burst and twisted back to see the guy get a faceful of sand. The other two looked fitter, and sped after him.

Jake now found an extra burst of speed. He could hear his pursuers panting. One of them was shouting into his walkie-talkie: 'Towards the lake! Towards the lake!'

Jake started to feel pins and needles creeping into the ends of his fingers. The security guards were dropping off. One bent over, hands on his knees with exhaustion. Jake slid down a bank to the lakeside. The fence was two hundred metres away, but there was another security guard running along the edge of the water towards him. Boats were stacked up in a line against each other by a jetty. Jake darted along the wooden boards, and then jumped on to the first boat. It lurched beneath his feet, but he managed to leap into the next. Then one more. The guard on the bank changed direction as Jake took a deep breath and dived off the last boat and into the cold water. He swam, pulling himself along with powerful strokes, eating up the distance to the far bank.

The guard had to go the long way round, and arrived as Jake was dragging himself out of the water.

'Stop!' the guard said, panting. From his belt, he pulled out a short baton. 'Don't make me use this!'

Jake heard footsteps on the other side, and realised one of the guards from earlier had caught up as well. 'Nice one,

Jim,' he said. 'You got a lot to answer for, kid.'

Jake felt a pain stab in his upper arm, and clutched his shoulder. It was like an electric shock spreading across his chest. There wasn't long left. With a lunge, he shoved the nearest guard in the chest, and sent him splashing into the shallows with a cry. The other guard, Jim, swung his baton. He heard it crack across his jaw, but barely felt a thing. Jim stared at him with wide eyes, and Jake dropped to a crouch and drove a fist into his thigh. The guard buckled with a dead leg and lay on the ground moaning.

Jake ran again towards the fence, water dripping off him. He threw himself at the mesh, and climbed quick as a monkey hand over fist. He dropped down the other side into the car park. A small girl beside a car tugged at her mum's elbow and gasped.

Jake sprinted to the main road. When he reached the street, he skidded to a stop and tried to get his bearings, but his body was a revving engine. He jumped to exert the energy that was building inside of him. Bolting towards town, he navigated by memory as he went. The pain lurched across his shoulder once more, and his heart seemed to clench. Black spots speckled his vision for a few seconds then faded.

Traffic was heavy, but Jake didn't stop to think – he continued in a straight line to his destination. He dashed across the busy street. Car horns seemed to blast from all directions at once, and a vehicle jolted to a halt with a screech just a metre away. Jake caught a glimpse of the driver's face, contorted with anger. A cop on the other side of the road stood with his hands on his hips, shouting abuse.

Jake faced the traffic head on and ran down the centre of the street. The car horns blasted, and drivers swerved either side or pressed their feet on the brakes. He heard screeches and shouts, and the clash of metal on metal as cars shunted into one another. Between the passing cars, he saw the cop running along the pavement, gripping his hat to his head with one hand and pushing his radio button with the other.

A car door opened in front of Jake, and an angry woman stepped out to stop him. Jake leapt up on to the bonnet of her car, and ran across the roof in pounding steps.

'Why, you little . . .' she called after him as he dropped off the other side and continued. Up ahead, the road dropped into an underpass. Jake didn't fancy going that way, so he climbed a steady incline. He guessed he'd run almost a mile since Dr Chow's lab. He wasn't even out of breath, but he knew his body must be suffering inside. The fire in his lungs seemed to drive him on rather than slowing him down.

From somewhere, his ears picked up the sound of sirens.

Seconds later, he caught the flashing blue lights coming from a road on the right. He reached a bridge over the underpass – at least a ten-metre drop. Another car swerved in from the left. They had him covered from both sides. One of the cars stopped and two cops jumped out, both with their guns drawn.

'Freeze!' one yelled.

The other car stopped as well. The black spots appeared again, stronger than before. He saw a truck dipping under the bridge. He didn't have a choice. With a yell of determination, he threw himself off the rail of the bridge. His legs wheeled in the air as he plummeted, landing on top of the moving lorry. He rolled, the world a blur, and managed to grab a securing rope before he fell off the side. Back on the bridge, the two policemen watched him in astonishment.

The truck driver couldn't have realised anything was wrong. He didn't stop. Jake crouched as the remaining blocks sped past. The truck pulled up at a corner Jake thought he recognised to stop at a red light.

Jake used the securing ropes to lower himself off the back, and landed in the road. The water on his skin had dried, but his clothes were sodden and torn. He heard sirens again, and ducked down a side street. It was quieter here and residential, with just the occasional shop. He passed a florist and convenience store, scanning for anything familiar.

Finally he saw it, two blocks down to his left. The green shamrock of Hannigan's. Almost there.

When he tried to carry on running, his legs seemed weaker. He stumbled against a rubbish bin. The lid landed on the pavement with a crash, and a dog started barking. Jake managed to stay on his feet, and he pressed onwards in an uneven jog, the black spots floating across his eyes like ink stains. His skin was suddenly hot, and sweat dripped into his eyes.

He practically fell through the door of the pub, weaving his way like a drunk towards the bar. Francesca was replacing a bottle over the rear counter.

'Jake?' she said, worried.

He didn't dare stop, and went through the door at the back.

'Hey, you can't just . . .'

Jake staggered on, steadying himself with his hands against the walls, and reached the end of the corridor. He yanked the grille aside, and stepped into the lift as Francesca came running after him. 'Wait, Jake.'

'Can't,' he said, his voice sounding strangely distant to his own ears.

He hit the down button, and watched her drift out of sight.

At the bottom, Jake had to use all his strength to pull the grille aside, and staggered along the corridor. Rick appeared in the doorway at the far end, swimming double then triple in front of Jake's eyes.

'What the hell do you think you're doing?' the scientist yelled. Jake sagged on to his knees. 'My god, what happened?'

Jake tried to stand, but couldn't. All his limbs seemed to have shut down, and all he could feel was his heart thudding. Rick arrived at his side.

'You've got to find out what's in me,' Jake mumbled. 'I drank it.'

'You did what?' Rick asked.

'Olympic Edge,' Jake gasped.

'But we already tested it,' Rick said. 'I found nothing. Oh Christ, what have you done?'

'This is different.' Jake's voice was a hoarse whisper. 'More potent. Please . . .'

'Don't talk.' He felt Rick pulling him upright, and draped his arm over the scientist's shoulders. He was half dragged into the lab, and laid in a chair. Jake focused on breathing. *In, out. In, out.*

'This may hurt a bit,' Rick said. 'Hold still.'

Rick's hand positioned Jake's head and he felt a stabbing in his neck, and the sensation of a needle probing deep under the skin.

'That should do it,' he said.

Jake could barely see a thing other than blurred grey shapes. He realised that Rick was moving quickly across the lab, and picked up the low beeps and clicks of a machine. He heard the CIA scientist muttering, but not the exact words.

The pins and needles, which before had been confined to his extremities, now seemed to assault his whole body in waves. Jake could do nothing as deep shudders spread across his chest. Rick was swearing, and then Francesca's voice called: 'Hold on, Jake. Hold on!'

As everything went black, Jake wondered if they'd be the last words he would ever hear.

21

Sounds, but he couldn't see anything.

A woman's voice: '. . . is it too late?'

'How the hell should I know?'

Jake blinked, and the world seemed too bright. He clenched his eyes closed.

'Jake?' He recognised Rick's voice.

He tried to mumble, 'Bright.' It came out slurred.

'Take it easy, Jake. Nice and slow.'

Jake managed to open his eyes a crack and saw Rick and Francesca standing over him. He moved his fingers, his toes. 'I'm . . . I'm OK.'

'Damn, kid!' Rick said. 'You had us scared.'

Jake shifted in the seat, and managed to sit up. His throat swam with nausea. 'I'm going to be sick.'

He felt a dish pressed into his hands, and Jake wretched violently, throwing up a huge spray of clear Olympic Edge and chunks of his breakfast.

'Better out than in,' Francesca said, rubbing his back. 'We gave you a concentrated emetic, and also something to slow your heart.'

'It took us an hour to put together an antidote,' he said.

Jake sat bolt upright, wiping his lips. 'I've been out for an hour?'

'Your pulse was up near two–fifty,' Rick said. 'We couldn't risk rushing things.'

Jake stood shakily.

'Whoa!' Francesca said. 'You're not going anywhere.'

'I need the antidote,' Jake demanded. 'My friend's going to die if I don't get it to her.'

Rick frowned. 'Someone else has taken that stuff?'

Jake nodded. 'Perhaps not the same concentration, but she's in hospital at the moment.'

'Jake,' Rick said. 'I'm still not quite sure what we're dealing with. What you swallowed, it was a damn *cocktail*. If I hadn't known what to look for – without all this equipment –' he waved his hand across the lab – 'you'd be dead right now.'

'That's why I need your help,' Jake said.

Rick sighed, and went to the counter. He took a syringe, and sucked up some fluid from a beaker, then corked the end. He handed it to Jake. 'Is there anything we can do?'

182

'Call my dad,' Jake said, taking his own waterlogged phone out of his pocket and dropping it in the bin. 'Tell him that Dr Chow is responsible . . . for everything.'

Back out on the street, Jake hailed a cab to the hospital, and said he'd pay double if they got there quickly. The driver obliged, cutting up other traffic and jumping a red light just as it turned. Jake apologised for the soaked dollar notes when he handed them over, but the driver didn't seem to mind.

As he hurried through the hospital corridors, Jake earned plenty of strange stares. He realised he must resemble an escaped mental patient in his bedraggled clothes and with a plaster taped across his neck where Rick had bandaged him after the injection.

A black doctor the size of a prop–forward barred his way. 'Where do you think you're going?'

'I need to see Veronika Richardson.' Jake pointed ahead. 'Room E12.'

'Are you family?' the doctor asked suspiciously.

'I haven't got time for this.' Jake tried to push past.

'Don't make me call security,' the doctor said, placing a solid arm in the way.

Jake fingered the syringe in his pocket. He was about to make a dash for it, when a Russian voice spoke behind him.

'It's about damn time!'

Igor Popov stood there with a bunch of purple and orange flowers. Even though the doctor was the size of both of them put together, Popov's voice seemed to carry a greater authority. 'He's with me,' Popov said, clapping a firm hand on Jake's shoulders.

'Sure thing, sir,' said the doctor, stepping aside and off along the corridor.

Popov ushered Jake towards Veronika's room. 'So?'

'I've got the antidote,' Jake said, tapping the syringe through his pocket.

They rushed through the hospital, dodging medical staff and patients.

'Veronika was conscious earlier. She was even able to walk a bit. I left her sleeping.' A great breath of relief left Jake as Popov's words washed over him.

'The doctor says she needs her rest,' continued Popov. 'Thank God you're here, Jake. The doctors still have no idea what caused this or how to help her.'

'Well, this should do the trick.' Jake walked beside his enemy to room E12 with a bounce in his step. Maybe this Olympic-size nightmare was finally over.

When they pushed the door open, however, Veronika's bed was empty.

Popov put the flowers on the bedside table and went to the bathroom door, which was half open. 'She's not here,' he said.

He stepped back into the corridor, and clicked his fingers impatiently. A passing nurse approached. 'Yes, sir?'

'The girl in here – my daughter,' he snapped. 'Where is she?'

'She was here a moment ago,' the nurse said, scanning the room.

Popov checked the cupboard. 'But all her things are gone,' he said.

'I'll alert security,' the nurse said, slipping away.

Popov turned back to Jake, muttering, '*Nyet. Nyet.*'

'What is it?' Jake asked.

For the first time since he'd met Igor Popov, Jake saw an expression of fear cross his face. The Russian ran a hand through his hair. 'She wouldn't have . . .'

'Wouldn't have what?' said Jake.

Popov looked up, panicked. 'The last time I saw her, we talked about what you told me, about Dr Chow being the one who's been killing athletes . . .'

'You think she's gone to confront her?' Jake asked.

Popov nodded, with a haunted expression in his eyes. 'She was angry, really angry. She said something about proving something to you, that she could be trusted.'

185

Popov turned from Jake and placed a call on his mobile phone. He tapped his fingers anxiously on the bed. Eventually he hung up. 'Jake, she isn't answering.'

'Don't worry,' Jake said. 'It's unlikely Dr Chow will try anything. She knows people are on to her.'

Popov picked up the bunch of flowers and hurled them across the room. Blooms scattered down the wall. 'You don't understand! It's not Dr Chow I'm worried about! She won't see tomorrow anyway.'

Suddenly Jake understood. Dr Chow had poisoned Popov's daughter. Of course the Russian wasn't going to let Chow live!

'What have you done?' Jake asked.

Popov sank on to the end of the bed. 'I've sent my people,' he said. 'They know what must be done.'

Jake gripped the Russian's shoulders, and shook him. 'Tell me!'

'They're going to kill Dr Chow,' he said. 'Then blow up the lab and everything in it.'

'And what if your daughter's in there?' Jake asked.

Popov's haunted expression told him everything he needed to know.

But it wasn't just Veronika's life at stake. It was his dad's too – Rick would have told him everything by now, and he'd be on his way to arrest Dr Chow.

'Call it off!' Jake shouted. Popov's hand was limply holding his phone.

'They won't have their phones on them,' Popov said. 'Not while they're on a job. Strict instructions – they must be untraceable in case they're compromised.'

Jake pulled Popov off the bed. 'We need to get to the complex – now!'

Popov seemed to shake himself out of his reverie. 'My car's outside.'

As they left the room, Jake held out his hand. 'I need to call my dad. Perhaps he can get there first.'

Popov looked momentarily unsure, then gave up his phone. Jake dialled quickly.

'This is Steve Bastin. Sorry I can't pick up at the . . .'

'Dammit!' shouted Jake, bringing glares from several of the people in reception. Two of Popov's suits stood up on cue. He waited for the recording to finish then left a message: 'Dad, listen to me carefully. Popov's rigged Chow's lab to blow. Make sure Veronika isn't in there!'

They climbed into the leather interior of Popov's 4x4 and the Russian barked an instruction to the driver in his native language. The vehicle lurched away from the parking lot with a screech of burning rubber, and pulled into traffic outside the hospital gates.

They cut across other cars, changing lanes with abandon and having several near misses. Popov kept shouting for the driver to go faster, and Jake clicked his seatbelt into place.

At the complex, the security barriers were down, and a security guard stepped out of his cabin. The driver pushed his foot on the accelerator and the 4x4 smashed through the bar, sending it spinning off to one side. Jake directed them to the medical centre and laboratories.

Popov was peering at his watch every few seconds, as if willing the seconds to tick slower. 'Not much time,' he said.

Jake was out of the door before the vehicle had even stopped, and running towards the entrance to the medical centre. His feet crunched on broken glass as he pushed inside. Last time he'd been here, he was running away with bullets flying.

'Veronika!' he shouted. 'Vron!'

The place seemed silent.

He ran along the corridor and into the main lab. Empty. Popov was somewhere behind him shouting his daughter's name. The Russian pushed into the rooms off each side, his normally greased-back hair hanging over his panicked face.

'Where is she?' he shouted. He pulled out his phone again, and quickly dialled. Seconds later, a faint tinkling tune answered somewhere above their heads.

'Upstairs!' Jake screamed.

He had one foot on the steps, when the whole building seemed to shift beneath his feet. A fraction of a second later, his eardrums felt the answering thud of an explosion and he was thrown back against the wall. It was like the sound of a car crash, only a hundred times worse. A pall of darkness spread over everything as smoke spread down the stairwell and dust and debris rained down on his head. The ceiling cracked, and began to fall. Instinctively Jake pushed Popov aside, and heard the Russian bellowing in the gloom. The ceiling sagged more, then collapsed with a roar. A huge section crashed down. Jake put up his hands to protect himself, thinking it could never be enough.

22

His body felt like a rag doll as the ceiling panels thundered down on top of him. He rolled into a ball to protect his head. It seemed to take minutes, but it could only have been a few seconds. He tried to suck in a breath, but there was no air, only thick smoke and dust. Bracing himself, Jake pushed upwards, and managed to reach a hand through the weight of debris on top of him. He cleared some room, twisting his neck to find something close to fresh air.

When he'd clambered up he saw his arms were streaked with blood. Above, fire crackled on the first floor. Not that there really were floors any more. Much of the ceiling had come down, and half the stairs had been blown out; the remaining portion hung perilously. Thunder-like percussions drifted from above.

Through the gloom, he saw shadows moving. Not Popov. These guys were dressed in shiny black body-suits, head to toe, with gas masks. One pushed past the other, and reached Jake. Even before he flicked back his mask, Jake knew it was his dad.

'Are you all right?' he shouted, helping Jake stand.

Jake nodded. 'Vron's upstairs.' His voice echoed in his head.

'We'll take care of it,' his dad said, steering Jake away.

Jake pulled back. 'It's my fault she's here,' he said. 'I'm not leaving her.'

'Steve!' shouted one of the other agents. 'We've got Popov.'

As soon as his dad turned, Jake went back to what remained of the stairs. Kicking a clump of flaming papers off the step, he picked his way up, using the wall as a support. Sprinklers had kicked in, sending out a fine spray that would never quench the devastation of such a large explosion.

'Come back!' called his dad hoarsely. 'It's not safe!'

Jake ignored him and reached the top. The first floor was laid out differently, with a large central hall surrounded by anterooms. Half the floor was gone, revealing wiring and steel girders, as well as charred joists. Gaps in the ceiling gave a view of clear daylight above. The furniture had been tossed, and scattered fires burned everywhere. It was hard to see anything at all in the shifting clouds of rolling black smoke. Heat baked his face. His dad was coming up the stairs behind him.

Across the other side was a room blazing more brightly than the rest – Dr Chow's private office. The partition wall wasn't there any more, and a few of the studs which had supported it were hanging loose. It was obviously the source of the explosion. Choosing bits of the flooring that appeared most secure, Jake navigated a path across the central hall. Fragments of broken lab equipment and burning tables blocked his way.

'Jake!' his dad yelled. 'This is suicide!'

Jake was almost there, but couldn't see Veronika anywhere. He allowed himself a second of relief. Maybe she wasn't here after all, but he had to be sure.

He placed his foot on what looked like a joist, but it gave way, and he plunged into the abyss below. His hands reached for anything and found the arm of a fallen office chair. It scraped across the ground and lodged in the gap. Jake's legs dangled into emptiness, but he managed to hold on, and drag himself back up. The smoke boiled thicker than ever. Struggling to see, he pulled his T-shirt up over his nose and mouth.

He glanced back, and saw his dad sticking to the edges of the room, coming carefully after him. A few more steps and Jake finally reached the office. He saw Dr Chow straight away. She was buried under a heap of ceiling masonry.

Her eyes were open and she was dead. Jake couldn't find any sympathy in his heart.

His eyes picked up a shock of blonde hair.

'Veronika!' he shouted, stumbling over. She too was lying beneath part of a fallen wall, her phone still clutched in her hand. Her eyes were closed and much of her hair had been burned away. Jake braced his legs and got his fingers under the section of plaster and wood that covered her. He heaved, and managed to toss it aside. But her legs were still pinned by a larger beam from the ceiling. Jake's eyes were watering so badly he could only open them for a second. He shook Veronika and shouted her name. She didn't move at all. Jake gripped the beam and pulled with everything he had to try to free her body, but it wouldn't budge. He pulled again, but this time lost his grip and fell back.

His dad dropped beside him, and felt Veronika's wrist.

Jake reached for her again, but his dad snaked a strong arm round his chest and held him back. 'She's dead, Jake!' he shouted. 'We need to get out of here.'

Jake fought against him. 'Let me go!'

She couldn't be dead. Not after all they'd gone through.

'Jake,' his dad said, pointing across the room where the flames were licking up alongside a pile of metal canisters. 'That's nitrogen. If it goes, everything goes with it.'

Finally, Jake's legs started to work. But as they reached the top of the stairs, the flames suddenly burst higher. Jake and his dad fell back, shielding their faces. There was no way down.

Jake scanned the blazing room. There was another door, off to the left.

'This way!' he shouted.

The door was locked. Jake took a step back, and slammed his shoulder into it. Not enough.

'Let me!' his dad said. He took a bigger run-up and the door splintered open with a crunch under his greater weight. They were in a tiny office with a window, undamaged by the bomb. Billowing smoke followed them in. Jake picked up a chair, and hoisted it over his head. He launched it at the window, and the glass exploded outwards. Jake climbed on to the sill, and helped his dad up beside him. Below, Popov's 4x4 was parked just off to one side. It was a long drop, but what choice did they have.

'Let's do it,' he said.

Jake jumped a fraction ahead of his dad, just as a second explosion lifted him from behind.

The air blasted through his hair as he fell, and his feet crunched on to the metal of the car roof, making deep dents. Jake rolled off, and tumbled to the tarmac. Smoke and dust spilled out over the road, and flakes of ash, caught on the wind, were carried off over the trees nearby. Jake saw his father sprawled over the bonnet of the car. He slid off weakly.

'Dad!' Jake rushed to his side, and turned him over. 'Dad!'

His father opened his eyes slowly, blinking. He stared up at Jake, confusion creasing his face. Another black-suited agent crouched beside them, his mask pulled aside to reveal a young man with ginger stubble.

'Are you OK, Steve?' he said.

His dad sat up slowly, and pointed to his ears. A trickle of blood stained his jawbone. 'I think my eardrums are busted!' he shouted.

The agent nodded, and together they helped Jake's dad to his feet.

'Will he be all right?' Jake asked.

'Should be,' the agent replied. 'Come on, let's get help.'

They rounded the corner, Steve Bastin limping for real, but came to a halt as they saw the true scale of the devastation. The front wall of the building had completely collapsed, revealing the chaotic mess of the interior. Fires blazed everywhere. His dad had been right: nothing could have survived the force of the gas explosion. Even Veronika's body would have been turned to ash.

A small team of the black-clad commandoes was surrounding Igor Popov and his men, their guns drawn. Popov himself was covered in soot, but otherwise unharmed. When he saw Jake, he lunged at him, eyes bright white in his dirt-streaked face.

'You!' he hissed. 'You killed her! You killed my little girl!'

His own men held him back, but Jake still thought he might break free. His mouth was flecked with spit as he cursed Jake, and the veins in his neck stood out like cords under his skin.

'You got her involved! You brought her into this!'

Jake broke away from his father, who tried to hold him back. He approached until he was only a metre away from Popov's straining face.

'You caused this,' Jake said, trying to keep calm. 'You planted the bomb that killed her, because you had to prove who was boss. Just like you had to finish Christian Truman and his son in St Petersburg.' He couldn't prevent his voice rising to a shout. 'Veronika would be alive if it wasn't for you.'

Popov roared and fought, but there was no way he was getting away from his men. 'Let me go!' he shouted. 'Let me go!'

They loaded him into the back of the 4x4. As they did so, he strained, shouting out: 'I'll hunt you down, Jake Bastin!

196

I won't ever stop coming after you. I'll kill −'

His voice was cut off as the doors slammed shut.

Sirens sounded in the distance. 'We have to vacate,' said the agent who'd helped Jake's dad. The others were already climbing into the back of a white van.

'We can't just leave her,' said Jake, pointing back to the building.

His dad tugged at his arm. 'We have to, son. Come on!'

The Rolex, encrusted with diamonds and platinum, the watch Popov had used to track him, sparkled on Jake's outstretched arm. The weight of it, what he'd done, what Popov had done to bring this fiery end was overwhelming. Jake ripped the watch off his wrist and hurled it into the burning rubble. He didn't want anything to remind him of the mess he'd made. Even without the watch, Jake knew Popov would hunt him down.

Jake's dad pulled him into the back of the van. Before the door shut they were speeding away. Distant sirens grew louder.

'There'll be a lot of explaining to do,' his dad said.

Jake leant back in his seat as they passed an approaching fire engine. He shut his eyes and saw Veronika's body lying crushed and surrounded by the debris of the lab. If only he'd been quicker. If only he'd figured it out sooner.

As he opened his eyes again, he felt the sting of tears. Not from the fire or the smoke, but from grief.

'I should have saved her,' he said.

23

When he drilled the ball into the bottom corner of the net in the thirty-ninth minute, Jake didn't celebrate, even though the crowd was going wild. He turned and jogged back to the halfway line, accepting the pats on his back from the rest of the team. Even Oz muttered, 'Great goal, Jake.' They were playing a defensive strategy and the Australian had agreed to drop back into midfield so Jake could play up front on his own. His sudden change of heart had been a surprise, but the last few days had put things into perspective for everyone.

A week ago, playing against the US team would have been a dream, but after what had happened that day at the lab, all Jake's senses seemed dulled. Krantz, grasping at whatever straws remained, had insisted that the game go ahead. They were all wearing black armbands, a symbol that this year's Olympic Advantage camp had been marked by tragedy.

The papers were already saying the same arrangement next year was unlikely. Jake hardly knew what to think.

As he waited for the restart, he took in the rest of the packed stadium. Sure, most of the people were here to see the US first eleven, rather than the successful squad picked from the camp, but there were plenty of scouts and journalists too. Jake saw a couple of the TV cameras trained on him, and had to tell himself this could be the start of something really special. But his heart wasn't in it.

The game restarted, and Jake's team were 3−1 down. Not bad against the professionals. He saw his dad standing on the sidelines, a bandage wrapped round his head. Only one of his eardrums had been properly perforated, the other was only bruised. He gave Jake a fatherly thumbs-up.

The explanations had been easier than expected. MI6 had leaked news of Dr Chow's testing to the police, and her death was still being investigated alongside the CIA. His dad had already assured him that the official finding would be an accidental death.

Another cover-up that got Igor Popov off the hook. Easier that, his dad said, than exposing MI6's involvement.

As the half-time whistle sounded, Jake trudged off the pitch with the rest of the team to the dressing room.

Camera flashes were going off everywhere, so he did his best to paste a smile on his face. He was at the back of the group as they entered the tunnel, and he felt a hand on his shoulder.

'Let's talk,' his dad said. He turned to his assistant. 'Jerry, can you take the team brief?'

'Sure, Coach,' Jerry said.

Jake's dad led him past the dressing room to a physio room. He held the door open, and gestured to the treatment table. 'Sit down.'

'I should be with the rest of the team,' said Jake, staying by the door.

'This is important.'

He took a seat, and his dad sat beside him.

'Your head isn't in the game,' said his dad.

'And why do you think that is?' Jake replied. 'There's more to life than football.'

'I know that,' said his dad. 'But you have to be able to separate things. This ninety minutes is about what happens on the pitch. It could be about your future.'

'I guess I can't forget about the past,' Jake said.

His dad sighed, and stood up, absently stroking a finger along the edge of his jaw. 'Jake, I regret every day I got you involved in all this.'

'Well, you did,' said Jake. 'And you just can't push me away now.'

'You need to take a step back,' said his dad.

'And let Popov get away again?' asked Jake.

His dad bristled. 'Jake, he's lost his daughter. He hasn't got away with anything. He'll be carrying the burden of that day for the rest of his life.'

Jake stood too. 'That's not enough, Dad, and you know it. Popov had never taken the slightest bit of interest in his daughter.'

'You need to deal with loss,' said his dad. 'It's part of life.'

Jake was tired of listening to it. He knew his father was right, but he just couldn't view Veronika as collateral damage. *We're not talking about losing a football game here*, he thought.

'You've proved yourself,' said his dad, wrapping his arms round Jake's shoulders. 'Both on and off the pitch. Maybe it's time to leave the spy work to the professionals, eh? Concentrate on your football.'

Jake looked into his dad's eyes. *Who knows what he's been through*, he thought.

'Maybe you're right,' he said.

'That's the spirit,' said his dad. 'Come on son, let's get back out there.'

Jake was still thinking about his dad's words in the second half. They managed to tighten up their defence, so the US team didn't get any more goals. In the ninety-first minute, Jake's side earned a corner, and Oz went up to take it. The Americans had all ten guys back behind the ball, and there was quite a bit of jostling in the box.

As Oz knocked the ball in, Jake felt a tug on his shirt, but managed to pull away. The corner was perfect. Pacy, with a slight curl outwards. Jake leapt into the air, climbing a fraction higher than the defender. He jerked his neck, and connected sweetly, directing the ball goalwards. A fraction of a second later, the defender collided with him, and he sprawled across the ground. The crowd's screaming told him he'd scored before he even saw the ball in the back of the net. One after the other, Jake's team-mates piled on top of Jake, all whooping with joy. The crowd's roars became like the sound of distant traffic.

At the bottom of the pile, Jake heard the final whistle go. They'd lost, but they'd fought to the end.

3–2 was a loss he could accept. Veronika was not. There was a lot more to life than football.

As Jake's team peeled off him, he remembered his last words to Veronika before she collapsed.

You're a liar. You're no better than your father. He'd been wrong. So wrong it burned inside. He'd never be able to take those words back.

But he could make amends. Popov had to be stopped. One way or another. Jake was prepared to do whatever it took to bring him down.